SAMURAI

Hisako Matsubara
SAMURAI

Translated from the German by Ruth Hein

Times
BOOKS

First published in 1978 as *Brokatrausch*
by Albrecht Knaus Verlag, Hamburg, Germany

Published by TIMES BOOKS, a division
of Quadrangle/The New York Times Book Co., Inc.
Three Park Avenue, New York, N. Y. 10016

Published simultaneously in Canada by
Fitzhenry & Whiteside, Ltd., Toronto

Library of Congress Cataloging in Publication Data

Matsubara, Hisako.
  Samurai.

Translation of *Brokatrausch*.
I. Title
PZ4.M4357Sam (PT2673.A67)   833'.9'14   79–51443
ISBN 0–8129–0852–X

Manufactured in the United States of America

Note to the Reader

Samurai takes place in the first decades of the twentieth century.

The Japanese word *yōshi* means "adopted son" but also more, a son to carry on the family name. Therefore, the adoption simultaneously involves the arrangement for the *yōshi's* future marriage, commonly with a family daughter.

The Japanese slang word *kimin* (literally "garbage people") here refers to Japanese who have emigrated from Japan, thus is a pejorative term, the *kimin* being condemned as virtual traitors, outcasts, scum.

SAMURAI

 # Prelude

As the sun slipped behind the cliffs, ever more people drifted to the shore, carrying Obon ships made of reeds, with high sterns and steep bows. Six men were needed to lug the largest ones, while two or four bearers sufficed for others. The mast of every ship was lashed tight between bow and stern with a sturdy sisal rope, and each bore a square sail on which thick black brush-strokes had inscribed a name.

Multicolored lanterns dangled from the lashing ropes or hung down from the dowels supporting the sails. None of them was lit yet.

"It isn't time," said a young man who, along with another man, was carrying a medium-sized Obon ship on his shoulders. They set it down carefully a few yards from where I stood, at the place where the sand shone wet and dark, tinged by the softly rolling surf.

"The tide isn't full yet, nowhere's near," an old man shouted to them from the rear. "It's been a long time since you idiots have been to sea."

"It's all right, old man," the young man called back. "We haven't lit the lanterns."

"But don't you know that the sea is still rising?" the hoarse voice at their back grumbled. "You have to set the boat down a few yards farther up the shore, or the souls will think the journey is about to start."

Laughing, the two young men tightened the belts around their short kimono jackets and smoothed out their loincloths. "All right, old man," they shouted and carried the soul ship a few feet farther up the sandy beach.

The crowd at the shore was still growing. Groups of women were coming from the town, children running ahead of them, passing each other and filling the air with bright laughter. A few children, who also carried ships like the adults, walked at a measured pace and complained when others drew too close to them.

"Watch out—you'll break my ship."

"Who did you build it for?"

"For my little sister. She died this year."

"I built mine for my grandma," another child called out. "She's been dead three years."

"May I go in the water?"

"No," a mother advised. "It's not time yet."

"You must wait for the moon," a sharp childish voice remarked self-importantly. "Otherwise the boats lose their way on the ocean."

"But they have their lanterns."

"They lose their way just the same," the same pedantic child's voice instructed.

"But the moon rose long ago," an older boy said. "Look. It's full and high on the horizon."

"That's true," said the old man. "But you're all blockheads.

The tide will keep rising for two more hours before it is at the full. We will not take leave of the souls until then."

"The wind is still blowing from the wrong quarter," a woman standing next to me said into the increasing darkness.

"It will shift soon," another woman answered, "and blow from the mountains."

Laughing and shouting, the shadowy shapes on the beach thronged together more and more closely. Here and there the man-high torches stuck into the sand all along the beach were already burning. Each roll of the surf seemed to light more torches, until a necklace of flickering, wavering flames was strung along the curving shore. The lights extended from the last houses at the harbor to the steep, dark cliffs at the end of the sandy beach. The torches' reflection also spotted the foam cresting on the shallow waves.

The shadows of the dancers surged back and forth. Rhythmic clapping came from every direction, accompanied by encouraging shouts. At first only the children had begun to sing, then the women joined in, and finally the men as they danced around the torches, stamping and swaying.

They sang of the pleasure of sensing the nearness of the souls for three days; they sang of this night, the night of leavetaking; they sang to say that the full moon was now high on the horizon to send its light along on the journey to the distant land. And always they sang the refrain:

> Return
> Next year
> Return . . .

"Now the tide is almost full," the old man's cawing could be heard again. "And the wind has turned in a favorable direction."

"Matches . . . matches . . ." a dozen children's voices cried out.

The flaming torches in the sand were now extinguished one by one.

I leaned down to my boat and lit both its lanterns. In their pale light I read the two names I had painted on the white sailcloth: *Nagayuki* and *Tomiko.*

I was pleased with my brushstrokes. I had succeeded in making them quite legible in spite of the unaccustomed thick, crude brush and the tacky oil paint on the rough cloth.

It is indeed an odd adventure, I suddenly thought, to come here—to Himari—where I have never been before, and to buy an Obon ship made of reeds with two lanterns and a white sail from an old net-mender who lives in a half-rotted house at the wharf wall.

When I had arrived in Himari and asked people where I might buy an Obon ship, everyone told me that the old net-mender at the harbor was the town's best boat weaver and that, besides, he knew how to attach a sail properly.

The old net-mender asked me what names I wanted him to write on the sail.

"None," I said.

"Don't you intend it for a dear departed?" he asked, looking at me in the way old people in a small town look at a young woman whose manner of speaking reveals that she is not from these parts.

"Yes," I replied, "for two departed souls. But I want to write the names on the sail myself. May I borrow a brush from you, and some paint?"

The old net-mender looked over my shoulder as I wrote. "No family name?" he asked, puzzled, when he saw that I wrote only *Nagayuki* and *Tomiko* on the sail.

"No," I replied.

"Weren't they married?" he asked.

"Yes, but . . ."

I did not want to tell him about these two. If I had, the old net-mender would have asked more questions, would have wanted to know what prompted me to fix up an Obon ship for these particular departed souls.

I tried to imagine this same man—not so old then—standing here at the harbor more than sixty years ago, a boy. He might have been one of the young fishermen at the dock who watched as Nagayuki boarded the ship that would take him to America. I wondered for a moment whether to ask him what it had been like when Nagayuki was carried here in a litter to board the ship. But then I would have had to tell him that I am Nagayuki's granddaughter. The news would have spread like the wind through Himari.

Finally there was nothing left for me to do but to gather the foods I meant to place in the Obon ship. Custom required that on their long journey back to the distant land, the souls be amply provided with those dishes they had most enjoyed in their lifetime.

I was reasonably sure about Nagayuki. After his return from America, he ate only three bowls of rice a day and with them a few slices of radish, over which he poured soy sauce drop by drop. When he ate the radish, he made a crackling noise as he chewed.

Everyone present noticed the crackling at the great banquet his relatives gave to celebrate his return. "How unusual for such an old man to still have such good teeth," someone at the table said softly. "I'm sure they are false."

"Yes, I think so, too. In America they make very good false teeth."

"But expensive, I've heard."

"Surely that's not a consideration for him. He must be very wealthy."

Nagayuki sat in silence amid the large circle of guests and did not seem to notice the covert, searching looks directed at him. He held his full rice bowl very steadily in his left hand, using his chopsticks carefully to pick up a small amount of rice. He seemed solemn as he chewed his rice. He appeared very rumpled and slight as he occupied the place of honor in front of the recess holding an insignificant scroll painting of Mount Fuji.

Because he was so silent, and because out of all the delicacies he helped himself only to a bit of radish and a small piece of grilled fish, someone at the table said that it would have been better if they had held the banquet in a restaurant with a Western menu.

"Probably he doesn't enjoy our food because in America he ate steak all the time."

Nagayuki looked up briefly and gave an embarrassed smile.

"How was it in America?" he was then asked in broken English. When he did not reply at once, the questioner continued, "Good or not good?"

Then Nagayuki, speaking softly but in a very mellifluous Japanese, said, "It is not easy to tell the space of sixty years in a few words."

All were impressed and nodded.

"So much has happened to him . . . He will probably write a book about his adventures."

"A book? What nonsense! I'm sure he could write ten books."

The conversation quickly came to the conclusion that everyone who had been in America or Europe even once had enough material for several newspaper articles and for interviews in front of the television cameras.

"And that brings in a lot of money—"

"Yes—enough to pay the costs of the trip."

That made all the relatives laugh and look at Nagayuki with a strange greed. The idea that in addition to the many dollars he must have brought back from America he could now easily earn untold thousands or even millions of additional yen heightened the general merriment. And so the after-dinner speeches jovially alluded to the five dented suitcases that were carried off the ship after Nagayuki. Everyone knew what had to be inside, the speakers said, for the shabbiness of the outer shell readily led to conclusions about the great value of the contents. Stock certificates perhaps, or dollar bills—bundles of them. After sixty years of America, one could hardly expect otherwise.

For as long as Nagayuki lived with us in our house in Kyoto after his return, he regularly and with extreme frugality ate only his three bowls of rice a day, accompanied by radishes and a little fish. If my mother, wishing to offer him something special, asked if he felt like a juicy steak, his voice always answered only, "No, Michi."

When I assembled the foods for my Obon ship, I reflected that Tomiko probably ate what Nagayuki ate. That is why I went to a store and bought boiled rice. With a little salt, which I sprinkled on my palm, I rolled it into balls and laid them on lotus leaves. As one does for the dead, I stuck the chopsticks straight up into the balls. I used other lotus leaves as plates for a bit of vegetables, radish slices, and two strips of grilled fish.

When the tide crested and even the last torches on the beach had been put out one by one, I made sure that my two lanterns were burning steadily, and in their glow I assured myself that all the foods were properly arranged on the lotus leaves. Finally I removed the lids from the two earthenware teapots, for, it is said, souls lack the strength to open the lids themselves.

After that I cautiously lifted up my Obon ship. I saw that most of the children who had Obon ships and many of the young men were already waiting in the water, and I followed them slowly. The deeper I stepped into the waves, the higher I raised my ship, to safeguard it from the first touch of water, which is the beginning of leavetaking.

Behind me on the beach, the children, women, and men sang their refrain in increasingly mournful voices.

Return
Next year
Return . . .

The oblong ovals of my ship's lanterns swayed back and forth, and their lights flickered. The soft ripples of the sand below the water caressed my bare soles. Finally I set my ship carefully down on the water, balancing it with both hands. As I turned the bow to the open sea, I felt the boat rising and falling in the surge of the waves.

Plunging ever deeper into the water, I waited for the wind, blowing from inland, to fill the sails; but the wind was still weak and irregular.

Farther out, other lanterns and small colored lamps were already swaying. Some young men, swimming alongside, were pushing a large Obon ship with ten or twenty lanterns and a fat barrel of rice wine as its most important cargo; they were driving it into ever-deeper water. They shouted to each other that they had gone far enough; the outgoing tide would take care of the rest. To the right and the left of me, too, innumerable boats and their lanterns were dancing on the dark water. As they swayed, they outlined the waves rolling softly and endlessly from the open sea into the broad bay.

The delicate colors of the lanterns glowed in the night, white or yellow, orange and red, with dancing reflections. Farther out to sea, the colors faded, and all seemed to be white, escorted by a seam of light on the crest of the waves.

With a last look at the dimly illuminated cargo of my boat, I gave it a long push and watched it move away from me.

I closed my eyes and folded my hands. I beseeched the waves to carry my ship on the outgoing tide into the open sea.

I beseeched the wind to blow more strongly from the hills, so that the sail with the two names might swell powerfully and my ship reach the horizon more quickly.

I beseeched the candles in my lanterns to burn a long time—if possible, all night long—and to light the way into the distant land.

I beseeched the wax-soaked paper to guard the candle flames against all froth and spray when, outside the protected bay, the wind pushed the waves higher, crowning them with foam.

I beseeched the stern of my ship not to dissolve in the salt water.

I beseeched the rope knotting the bundles of reeds not to loosen before it was time.

I beseeched the moon not to hide behind clouds.

When I opened my eyes again, my ship had already gone some distance from me. Other ships with their lanterns drifted past me. I felt the sluggish tow of the outgoing tide and dug in my feet to resist it.

Only a few lanterns were still bobbing in the space between me and the edge of the beach. The sand stood out gray against the darker background of the crowd, now standing silent and motionless.

When, a little while later, my eyes searched for my ship again, I could no longer tell it apart from the others. On the expanse of the horizon, thousands of lights danced and floated, those closer by showing their colors, those in the distance only white. They flickered among the waves' crests.

Soon there were no more lanterns on the water that were any brighter than the moon's reflection mirrored on the waves.

And then the lanterns of the Obon ships merged into a single ribbon of light. Like glowing plankton, it dissolved on the ocean.

I turned around and walked back up the beach.

1

The decision that Nagayuki would go to America was made in a single night.

The weather was close and hot. All the shoji screens in the house stood wide open, so that the wind could course through all the rooms. But the air hung still and heavy over the whole town. Even the sea brought no relief. From all sides the shrill, piercing sound of the crickets cut and snipped the air with its high treble.

Tomiko had already retired. Since their return from Tokyo she had not felt well. She attributed her recurrent nausea to the long, exhausting trip through the glimmering plains of the Tokaido route, past the steep slopes and along the sea. In the tunnels, too, the air had remained sticky and hot.

Then they had arrived in Himari, where the subtropical force of the heat acted like a glass bell to trap the dust and the odors of the town in the streets.

Even the pines in the grounds surrounding the Hayato mansion and the closely ranked bamboo thickets at the edge of the pond, fed by the hot springs from the rocks far behind the house, could not filter out the town smells. At best, the sounds were so muted that even during those rare moments when the crickets and the cicadas fell silent, the noises were hardly more audible than the murmur of the surf along the distant cliffs on the other side of the harbor.

Tomiko brushed aside the idea that she might be pregnant with an incredulous smile. She blamed the closeness of the day for her sense of malaise and her physical weariness. She longed to be back in Tokyo.

In Tokyo she and Nagayuki had been alone for three years. They had been free, and she had encountered many things that she could barely have imagined during her childhood and school years in Himari. In Tokyo electric streetcars already moved along on iron tracks and no longer required horses to pull them. On the Ginza there were hardly any old houses left. Everything had been pulled down in recent years and built up anew in the Western style, with red brick walls and pillared arcades. Many buildings even had balconies, where the people could stand and look down on the passersby in the street.

Nagayuki had bought a hip-length black cape, lined in scarlet. When he walked ahead of Tomiko, and when the wind was blowing hard, one or the other corner turned back, letting Nagayuki appear like a rushing temple-door keeper, sheathed in flame. At those times Tomiko was proud of Nagayuki because he was beginning to free himself from the rigid conventions that had shaped their youth in Himari and to develop his own style.

The simple fact that she and Nagayuki could go all over the huge city and never meet anyone they knew had been a whole new experience for her; and she had thought that Nagayuki, too, must have been pleased by the absence of the ever-present gossip of the people of Himari. The freedom of the big city, which at the beginning had frightened her a little, spread its protective veil over her. She felt that under the protection of anonymity she could grow closer to Nagayuki—a little closer every day. When the three years were up, the time seemed to have been too short.

She liked thinking back to the afternoons she had spent in the large stores on the Ginza, where the most beautiful kimono fabrics she had ever seen were spread out under glass. More than the kimonos, however, she was fascinated by the Western clothing that was beginning to appear occasionally on the streets. Tomiko had also seen many white women with very blond hair. Their arms and shoulders were bare. Their skin was a pale pink, and they walked in narrow, pointed shoes.

Tomiko had bought a large triangular shawl of Brussels lace. She sewed her own European clothes from thin, light silk, using patterns from a fashion magazine. Nagayuki's astonishment when she modeled her first dress for him—a dream of white silk with puffy sleeves and a very small waist—was enormous.

"We'll take the dress to the theater tomorrow—we'll give it an outing right away," Nagayuki said, caressing her with a smile. After the way he had spoken while looking at her so tenderly, she felt intensely proud the following night when she wore the tight-fitting European silk dress. Copying what she had seen the white women do, she tossed the lace shawl around her shoulders. All Himari would be aghast, she thought to herself, if she were to turn up there dressed like this.

Tomiko's mother softly entered through the open sliding door, lifted up the mosquito netting, and slipped through it. She sat next to Tomiko. She fanned cool air in her daughter's direction.

"You haven't told us much about Tokyo yet," her mother said.

Tomiko turned her head to one side, where the night sky stood out faintly against the shadowy-black pillars of the doorposts. The few stars whose light was able to pierce the trembling, hot layers of air over the town shimmered reddish-yellow. Seen through the mosquito netting, they were surrounded by a corolla whose points of light seemed in ceaseless motion.

"You've brought a new hairstyle back from Tokyo," her mother started once more. "It's very becoming to you."

Then they were silent again, each lost in her own thoughts.

Somewhere in the house the measured, firm voice of Father Hayato was raised in the darkness. "Nagayuki, come here."

Nagayuki's restrained, almost shy footsteps scraped over the tatami matting.

"Is Nagayuki good to you?" her mother asked. Tomiko nodded.

After a long pause, her mother continued. "You had a hard time of it in Tokyo after Father stopped being able to send you so much money."

"It wasn't the money." Tomiko's voice was low.

Her mother waited in silence. She wanted to ask—but did not dare—whether Nagayuki had not been good to her. In the dark she searched for Tomiko's hand and stroked it gropingly, as if to make sure that the girl's skin was still as delicate and cared for as she wanted her daughter's to be, or whether it had roughened from too much housework.

"At the end, you were able to keep only a single maidservant. I often thought about all the work you had to do yourself."

"I would have preferred living in a single room without a maid . . ." Tomiko's voice sounded sulky and brusque.

"But you're not reduced to that!" her mother flared up, letting go of Tomiko's hand. "We are not that poor."

"Nagayuki didn't mind my wanting to go to school as well. He even agreed that it was a good idea. I could have enrolled at Tsuda College anytime. I could have studied English or literature. Three years would have been long enough for me to take my final exams. Then I would not have the feeling now of sitting around uselessly for three years without doing anything really meaningful. Nagayuki agreed, but you did not want me to study."

Tomiko spoke the last few words almost tonelessly and broke off without lowering her voice.

16

"I was told that once you wrote to Father about it," her mother said soothingly.

"I wrote more than once," Tomiko interrupted.

"But surely you weren't serious! You don't need to study—you are already married."

"I always wanted to study, whether I was married or not. In Tokyo I had the time and the opportunity—instead of running three maidservants and a wastefully large house. But you did not want me to."

"As the daughter of the house of Hayato, you cannot live in a single room, without household staff," her mother said, and she almost seemed to be begging for understanding. "If the word had gotten out in Himari that you lived that way in Tokyo, and that you were studying as well, the people would have thought we were in need."

After the first fever of the metropolis had passed, Tomiko had quickly grown bored in her large five-room home. Three servants looked after the house and the garden; there was nothing left for her to do.

The feeling of being unfulfilled was familiar to her from her school days in Himari. That was why, besides school, she had taken additional instruction offered to upper-class girls—tea ceremony, flower arranging, playing the koto, and calligraphy. Her teacher characterized her brushmarks as masculine in their vigor, and it was said of her touch that she revealed an even balance and a natural sense of elegance.

When she arranged flowers, too, her skill and her taste aroused universal admiration. Once, for a large reception, Tomiko had arranged unusually large grass clusters, a maple branch with bright red leaves, and chrysanthemums into a composition that reached to the ceiling. She called her arrangement "Dying Autumn." It won the first prize of the prefectural commission. Every day for all her school years she applied the same sure hand to shaping attractive compositions of flowers, branches, and twigs for the tokonoma recess in the Hayato home, where a particularly beautiful scroll painting or a calligraphic ornament hung at all times.

Father Hayato laid great stress on the care of the tokonoma recess, for there, as he pointed out in conversation time and again, the aesthetic center of the home was to be found. He loved taking care of the recess himself. Forming the northeast corner of the large reception room, it was slightly raised and flanked by two wooden pillars left in their natural state. For each season father selected the appropriate scroll. During the short transition periods, when spring turned into summer, summer into autumn, autumn into winter, and winter back into spring, he exchanged the scrolls for calligraphic designs which gave poetic form to the imminent changes in nature.

Father liked to see Tomiko helping him with maintenance of the tokonoma recess. He taught her that it must be kept absolutely free of any speck of dust, nor were any dead insects to be tolerated; the flowers placed there must be watered with the utmost care. He watched Tomiko with approval as she handled the flowers and twigs skillfully, and he praised her for so quickly grasping his admonitions to concentrate on the essentials. Only rarely did he criticize her color composition or the shape, so quickly had Tomiko learned to master the rules of this art. When guests came, Father Hayato could not conceal his pride and pointed out with well-chosen words that it had been Tomiko who, all alone, had assembled the flower arrangement in the tokonoma recess.

Nagayuki was never as clever in artistic matters. Father had realized this quite soon and had entrusted Nagayuki with those tasks that he considered suited to the boy's talents. Hayato instructed Nagayuki in the art of dwarfing young trees through the appropriate pruning of roots and branches. Under the father's direction, the boy had to cultivate bonsai trees.

Besides, Hayato placed great value on Nagayuki's ability to recite from memory all the maxims by which a samurai was to

18

measure his life. As these maxims filled eleven volumes, there was no end to learning.

Nagayuki was small-boned and seemed almost fragile. Though his outward appearance did not coincide at all with the harsh aphorisms he was learning by heart, nevertheless Nagayuki was eager to accomplish the task because Father Hayato was such a great example to him that he wished to emulate and someday even equal him. He worked very hard to please Father Hayato and to acquire for himself the strict standards of a samurai. Even when he went to Tokyo, Nagayuki had taken along the eleven volumes of samurai wisdom and leafed through them frequently.

Tomiko smiled to herself. She remembered how often, after they had spent an intoxicatingly wonderful evening together at the theater or a pleasant afternoon in the city, in shops or at a café, Nagayuki seriously clutched his printed samurai lore, recalling the higher meaning of life to his mind.

"The road of the samurai is straight," he would murmur, and Tomiko resisted the temptation to add what she had heard a thousand times: "High spirits rip open graves, and joy strews stones in the path."

Instead, in order to entice Nagayuki away from his absorption in the wisdom of the samurai, she said, "Your black-and-red cape flutters around you like a ring of flame."

"Really?" he asked, looking up in surprise.

"Yes. You stride through the streets like a temple guard. I can't take my eyes off you."

"Soon it will be summer," Nagayuki said. "Then the time to wear a woolen cape will be over."

"The night is hot." Her mother's voice rose timidly in the darkness. "I am glad that you are back."

"I am too," Tomiko answered softly and did not know if she was telling the truth.

2

Even before Nagayuki bent down to raise the mosquito net at the sliding door which hung down like a curtain before the open shoji, he could make out Father Hayato's outline. For three years Nagayuki had thought about him every day. For three years he had carried within himself the image of this man whom he had been allowed to call Father since the age of twelve and who, on the day when Nagayuki married Tomiko, had doubly become his father. During all his student days in Tokyo, Nagayuki had felt deeply indebted to Hayato. He wished to honor him and the family name by becoming the best student in his class. When, at the end of the first year, he was able to report to Himari that he had passed the year-end examination as eighteenth in a class of one hundred and twenty-five, he had secretly promised himself to do better the following year.

At the end of the second year—just when the depressing news had arrived that his father had suffered heavy financial losses

20

and would be sending only half the monthly sum he had contributed until now—Nagayuki was proud to be able to write home that he had become the third-best student.

In his final year, Nagayuki outdistanced all the others and was awarded his law degree with highest honors, the head of his class.

Father Hayato silently pointed his folded fan at the square floor pillow placed before him on the tatami mats. Clearly he had counted on Nagayuki's arrival and had laid the pillow in readiness. Nagayuki sat down with his legs crossed under his body and bowed slightly. He tried to sit straight and nobly, his back as concave as his father's.

The white mosquito netting all around captured the last light of the night sky and filled the room with gentle darkness.

Hayato carefully opened his fan again and moved the coolness in Nagayuki's direction, acting without haste and with much dignity. Each of his movements reminded Nagayuki of the special love his father harbored for the Noh theater. Each day Hayato spent at least an hour practicing Noh dancing and recitation. He was so steeped in this classical dramatic art that even his most ordinary gestures reflected the rigor of the ancient Japanese theater form. For Hayato, Noh was the art appropriate to the samurai, and he tried to adapt his life-style to it. When he walked through the house, he placed his feet according to a carefully calculated rhythm and moved gracefully and silently, almost floating through the rooms. In life as on the stage, he loved creating the impression of suppressed passion.

Father Hayato brooked no contradiction—ever—but he knew how to cloak his inflexibility in benevolence. He never gave orders in curt tones, but his mere presence prevented anyone in his household from even thinking of wishing to act in any way that he did not consider proper.

He considered the ability to make rapid decisions—an essential element of his samurai nature—and believed unshakably that these quick decisions had always been correct. But he never tormented himself or those around him with reproaches when the decisions led to disappointment instead of to success.

That was how, while Nagayuki was in Tokyo during the second year at the university, Hayato had lost almost half his fortune. A stranger who called himself a geologist had been able to persuade Hayato that a rich vein of gold had been found on one of the uninhabited rocky islands on the other side of a spit of land owned by the Hayato family for many generations. The stranger showed him gold-laced rocks and submitted written opinions from professors confirming that what he was looking at was genuine gold. Overwhelmed by the feeling of owning an island where gold had been discovered, and overcome by the integrity of the stranger—who was honest enough to tell him, the rightful owner of the island, of his find instead of prospecting for his own gain—Father Hayato at once appointed him mining engineer and ordered him to exploit the gold mine. The very next day, he handed the stranger the sum the man had, speaking in a very businesslike way, stated would be necessary to construct the mine and extract the gold from the rock. Hayato gave the stranger the money in cash. On his word of honor.

"And how is the political situation in Tokyo?" Hayato now inquired of Nagayuki without stopping his fan.

"The annexation of Korea is a certainty."

"Yes, I read as much. The samurai spirit prevails. Greater Japan is no longer an empty phrase, but a living reality. And there will be economic consequences as well."

"The Manchurian Railroad is being extended. They say there are huge coal beds there."

"I know. Manchuria is important for the economy, but our future lies on the other side of the Pacific. A samurai who loves his country must be open to the world."

"There's talk that a new trade agreement with America will be concluded."

"Yes, a new era is dawning. Many young people are going to

America. And the best of them return with great riches."

Nagayuki hesitated, wondering whether to talk of the offers he had received following his exceptionally good final examination. Tomiko was already dreaming of going to America with him. To San Francisco or even to New York.

"I—" Nagayuki faltered and began again. "I have a prospect of starting with Mitsui. Or of joining the Mitsubishi Shipbuilding Company or Toyo Textiles or the Yokohama Bank. All of them want me, and they want to send me to America soon. I don't know which one to take. I beg you to tell me how I am to decide."

His father remained silent, and even the fan came to a standstill.

"Tomiko has also learned English pretty well," Nagayuki added, to make their father doubly proud. "She can come with me."

"A samurai is not dependent on the help of women," Hayato replied, faint displeasure coloring his voice. His fan began to wave again. "Besides, the pay offered by Japanese firms is extremely low. Unworthy of a Hayato."

Now it was Nagayuki who fell silent. He would have liked to tell his father what the people from Mitsui, from Toyo and the Yokohama Bank had promised him. Because his command of English was unusually fluent, and because he could attest to that fact with a certificate from an American professor, they were prepared to send him abroad after a mere one-year training period. The foreign salary they promised seemed to him so ample that it made his head spin. If he translated the sum back into yen, he arrived at a salary greater than that of a Japanese governmental minister. The passage would also be paid for by the firm or the bank. Even Tomiko's.

Earlier, Nagayuki had planned the words he would use to tell his father about the possibilities open to him now that he had finished his studies, now that he had reached the top of his class at the university. All there was left for him to do now was accept one of the offers.

Tomiko and he had thought it over together, and on the trip from Tokyo to Himari they had talked about how much money they could save if they lived in America for three years. The sum they arrived at might be sufficient to make up for the losses their father must have sustained this last year. But of course Nagayuki could not raise the topic of his father's unfortunate reverses during their initial conversation. His father might find it offensive to be reminded. That was why Tomiko, too, had counseled caution and had impressed upon Nagayuki the need not to speak precipitately, not to say something that could serve to reopen a wound that was surely not yet healed over.

What Nagayuki did not know—and could not know—was the extent to which the Hayato fortune had shrunk. The little left to his father now threatened to vanish altogether, after an astonishingly hasty decision had made him a partner in a newly established shipbuilding firm. Someone from Osaka had figured out for him that the many trees growing in his forests outside Himari would render millions in profit if they were to be used to build huge oceangoing vessels, to be used in trade with America. Father Hayato had already had extensive sections of his forests cut down and the logs shipped to Osaka. But Osaka—where, as he knew, the ships were to be built—still had not sent word that the ships had been launched and were on their way to America with precious cargo.

No one told Hayato that these days oceangoing freighters were no longer built of wood, but of steel. The only news from Osaka came when the banks sent the first demands for the interest on the capital that the shipbuilding firm had so lavishly received.

When Father Hayato's voice suddenly cut through the darkness again, it sounded almost like a distant rumble. Soft at first, then increasingly loud and more decisive, Father Hayato spoke about

hat Hayato was looking for a yōshi, for his ow
ad given him no sons. Father Hayato had no grea
or the Ogasawaras. As a samurai, he could not hel
e them. All sword-carrying samurai saw the cour
a collection of weaklings.

ss, Hayato had adopted Nagayuki as a yōshi, thus
m the future bearer of the Hayato name. And
future husband. The final balance had been cast by
fine accomplishments in school. Her father wanted
he best man for Tomiko. Nagayuki was small-boned.
by his flawless manners, which attested to his good
g. There was nothing rough about him. Thus
fulfilled all of Hayato's requirements. If there was one
er Hayato missed in him, it was the toughness that the
-in-law of a samurai should have possessed.

e in Himari said, "The Honorable Hayato made the
when he took in Nagayuki."
er Nagayuki and Tomiko appeared together, they
lances of admiration.
tiful couple, even when they were children," the
the street said. "Hayato's daughter and Hayato's

ad long, curved eyes. Her irises were of such a deep
t they seemed almost black. In her narrow, pale, and
e her eyes seemed overly large and glowing. Tomiko's
were slight, and her hands were slender and supple.
its were especially apparent in Noh dancing. Her
e her lessons almost daily. Nagayuki, not a good
nself, was allowed to watch. Early on, he admired the
Tomiko's movements. It seemed to Nagayuki that
dancing was the most lovely thing he had ever seen.
ayuki also suffered from Tomiko. He suffered from

the decay of the old values. "It used to be that a samurai was strong alone. When a samurai directed his steps through alien soil, all dangers were held in check. The proud consciousness of inflexibility lent him power and assurance. It was his will that made a samurai invincible."

Hayato listened to the sound of his own voice dying away in the darkness.

"Today," he began anew and seemed to direct his voice toward Nagayuki, "today the sons of the samurai throng the portals of banks and large corporations—as if they needed protection. They rush into the banks and the large corporations and take their places behind desks. There they are anonymous. What kind of samurai are these, who believe that they must show a calling card, so that the name of the bank, or of the firm in which they have taken refuge, will cast a last vestige of honor on them?"

Never before had Nagayuki heard Father Hayato speak so vehemently. In the stillness of the night, the words became tinged with a note of menace. The darkness no longer swallowed the words but threw them back at Nagayuki.

Nagayuki bowed slightly to his father. He did not know what answer he might have made or whether he would be allowed to speak at all. His father's words seemed atrocious. The young man saw the banks and the large corporations in quite another light. To him they paved the way for a modern Japan. Long before the country opened to the world, Mitsui and Sumimoto had already assembled all the provinces into a single market. They were strong and dominated the country. It was they, too, who assisted in the overdue demise of the old order. With the weight of their capital they supported the establishment of imperial power. In recognition of this forward-looking wisdom, they—and the other concerns that had arisen in the intervening years—were granted monopoly rights for manufacture and trade. In this way the early beginnings developed rapidly into an efficient economy and industry, unique in the Far East. Less

25

her superiority. If the conversation was about school, he knew that, by comparison with Tomiko, his position was weak. Everything came easily to her. He had to work for everything. He was a hard worker. He threw himself into fields of knowledge in which Tomiko expressed no interest. There he gained the feeling that he did not have to avoid comparison with her. From early on he was fascinated by the history of foreign countries. He wanted to know the names of the cities, their size, the rivers and mountain ranges in the various countries, the kinds of rocks of which these mountains were made and whether they contained ore. He wanted to know how the winds blew, the tides ran, where the deserts were located, how thick the ice grew at the poles. Soon Nagayuki could recite the principal ports of every country, the goods transshipped at each, how the railroad lines ran that brought the goods to the ports, and the routes taken by the ships in their ocean crossings.

With all this, Nagayuki did not forget that he was a yōshi and that he must never relax his efforts to become a worthy bearer of the Hayato name. He wished to prove to his father that he was a good son and had fully absorbed the spirit of the samurai.

That was why Nagayuki trembled when, in the darkness, he heard his father's firm, clear voice saying, "You will go to America to bring greatness to the name of Hayato."

He did not understand what his father meant.

Silently and respectfully, he waited to hear the details of how he was to bring greatness to the name of Hayato in America. Perhaps Father had made connections with other firms or provided a diplomatic career for him. Perhaps he was even to accompany a minister on a visit of state.

Hayato continued to fan cool air toward himself, his motions unvaried and even. After a time, which seemed almost unbearably long to Nagayuki, Father Hayato once more repeated his decision: "You will go to America."

Then—deliberately—he added a single word: "Alone."

In the dark Nagayuki sensed his father's turning toward him. When it spoke, the voice was warm and kind. "Can you fulfill my wish?"

Nagayuki concealed his secret fear and forced himself to reply. "Yes, I can."

3

Tomiko did not go to say good-bye. Her mother had had a new
kimono made for her, in carefully muted autumnal colors—
ochre, beige, and deep purple—but also glowing little yellow
chrysanthemum blossoms, for Tomiko was still young, just
twenty. At her age she was still allowed to wear such bright
prints.

When the day of Nagayuki's departure arrived, it was
impossible to make up Tomiko's face for the ceremonial
leavetaking. Time and again, tears mingled with the white
powder which her mother, with the help of a maid, was trying to
apply to Tomiko's face.

All of Himari talked about Hayato's yōshi and his departure for
America. Five freight rickshaws had been engaged to take his
baggage to the harbor. They were already lined up before the
house. Porters carried out the large black lacquered chest inlaid

with mother-of-pearl and set it down on the valuable red felt rug that covered the floor of the first rickshaw.

The second rickshaw was made to hold the heavy wooden trunk, tightly wrapped in wax paper against the damp, which contained the many silk kimonos Nagayuki was to take to America with him.

The third rickshaw was needed for the books packed in cartons tied with rope.

Even on the fourth and fifth rickshaws, the cases, boxes, and packages were piled so high that it was not easy to keep them from toppling.

The rickshaw men in their black-and-white-checkered cotton jackets stood between the shafts, their backs bent, keeping a tight hold on the handles. Like horses, their legs, bare to the hips, pawed the ground intermittently to rest their feet, wearied by long waiting.

A large number of Hayato relatives, as well as members of the Ogasawara clan and especially Nagayuki's own mother, had gathered at the Hayato mansion to accompany Nagayuki to the Omiya shrine and to go with him from there down to the harbor. At the Omiya shrine a litter stood waiting; the highest honor that could be accorded Nagayuki was to have him carried for the last lap of the way. Because of these extraordinary events, the Himari town council had decided to close all the schools for the day, so that the children, along with the many other curious onlookers who were expected, could line the path of the procession. A small part in this decision was due to guilty consciences; for Hayato had until recently been Himari's municipal treasurer, and many town councillors had had time to regret his removal from office.

"What will the others think when they see you with tearstained eyes?" her mother said.

"I'm not going," Tomiko insisted. But her mother paid no attention and continued dressing her.

32

"I'm not going," Tomiko repeated. "And I don't want Nagayuki to go, either."

"But he'll be back in a year."

"I want to go with him."

"You can't do that now that you are pregnant."

Tomiko fell silent and passively allowed the dressing to continue.

"A year goes by quickly." Her mother tried to console her. "Once your baby is born, you won't be thinking of your husband anymore. It's always that way."

"I don't want him to leave," Tomiko repeated.

"But he'll come back in a year—or even six months—and he'll be bringing millions of dollars. Father said so."

"I don't want millions of dollars," Tomiko shouted at her mother, shaking her shoulders. "I don't want Nagayuki to leave."

Her eyes, brimming with rage and tears, seemed unnaturally large. Their corners were drawn higher than usual, almost reaching her temples. "I don't want it to happen."

Mother ordered the maid to run quickly to Father Hayato and tell him that Tomiko would be unable to join them. "Tell him it's because of the pregnancy—so people won't talk," she added. Tomiko bit the sleeve of her new kimono and ripped open the seam.

"Stop that!" her mother ordered, but Tomiko would not listen. Her ears were filled with the crackling and bursting of the fireworks which had been set off the night before to allow all of Himari to celebrate Nagayuki's journey to America.

"Hayato's yōshi is going to America," the people in the town said as they enjoyed the splendid fireworks. The subsequent banquet in the Hayato mansion seemed never-ending. Everyone thanked Hayato for the breathtaking flowers of fire in the night sky. When he returned, dressed in brocade, the town would set off fireworks for him.

"And that's not all," one man exclaimed. "We will erect a monument to him."

Father Hayato nodded in approval. The high hopes that all Himari placed in Nagayuki filled him with pride.

Mother had her hands full in the kitchen preparing all the dishes and beverages the guests were served. Five maids were kept busy without letup carrying in bowls of various foods and refilling the empty sake decanters with hot rice wine. The banquet went on until well after midnight.

Father and Nagayuki were seated on silken pillows in the mansion's large reception room. The room could hold forty persons sitting far enough apart so that they could just touch each other with outstretched arms. The center of the room remained empty. Flat serving tables, lacquered a dark red, stood before each place. The highest-ranking guests were assigned places near the tokonoma recess. Father and Nagayuki assumed the lowest-ranking places, at the opposite end of the room.

Nagayuki went from guest to guest, sat down in front of each on the tatami mat, and personally filled each one's sake bowl. Every guest emptied his bowl at one draft and then offered it to Nagayuki. Making a deep, polite bow, Nagayuki took the bowl, held it at eye level with both hands, and waited until the guest filled it. Then he emptied it in one gulp. With pleasure Hayato noticed that for the entire drinking round Nagayuki maintained his noble bearing and in his demeanor compared favorably with the townspeople, whose flushed, perspiring faces began to reveal the effects of their celebration.

Most of the guests had never been to Tokyo. Anyone who had ever taken a trip to the prefectural capital was already considered a world traveler. No one had been to a university. That Nagayuki had not only attended Japan's greatest university, the Todai, but had even brought back a gold-framed diploma, which sported the large red seal of the Imperial University—all that went beyond the comprehension of the people of Himari.

34

Father Hayato had had Nagayuki's diploma framed and hung on the wall in the reception room, in a spot where every visitor could not help but notice it. It gave Hayato profound satisfaction to see the townspeople so deeply impressed.

He had never recovered from the fact that after that unfortunate affair with the gold mine, which had lost him almost half his fortune, the town council had dismissed him from his office of treasurer. When he had been rich and in a position to be generous, he had several times made considerable donations to the town. And whenever there had been a hole in the municipal treasury, without wasting an unnecessary word on the matter, Hayato had filled it out of his own pocket.

When he himself had run into financial difficulties, he had expected to fall back on the communal coffers with the same matter-of-factness with which he had been used to help the town out of all previous straits. But there had been a huge scandal as a result.

The Himari newspaper reported that Hayato was guilty of embezzlement and misappropriation of public funds.

A meeting of the municipal council was hastily convened. Throughout the proceedings, Hayato spoke not a single word in answer to the many questions. He merely sat upright, his elbows at an angle, gazing with immobile mien at the picture of Meiji Tenno over the entrance portal.

When the vote revealed a majority in favor of his immediate dismissal from the office of town treasurer, he had risen to his feet, had looked sharply and searchingly at each man in the assembly hall, and had walked wordlessly to the door. The beadle did not know whether he should hold the door for him. But Father Hayato remained standing, head raised high before the closed door, until someone behind him in the room gestured to the beadle to open the door one last time for the dismissed municipal treasurer.

"Not just a monument," called a guest, his voice tipsy. "When the honorable son of the Hayato family returns, he will surely wish to donate something marvelous to our town."

"We already have a new judo hall," another said cheerfully. "It was a gift from the son of old Eda. He surely came back from America handsomely dressed in brocade."

"And yet old Eda is just a simple dockworker, and his son did not even finish elementary school."

Several glanced covertly at Father Hayato, for everyone knew that after his return from America, Eda's son had acquired several pieces of land which Hayato had had to liquidate in a hurry. And on one of these properties, where a profitable orange grove used to stand, the son of Eda built himself a large house in the Western style, six pillars marching across its front. There he sat all day long on the cool stone floors while his cat sprawled in the rocking chair which he had brought back from America and which he always placed by his side when he sat in front of his front door.

Hayato smiled self-confidently and watched Nagayuki with unconcealed pride.

"There's no comparison at all!" someone in the circle said quickly. "A dockworker's son and a Todai graduate. From such a great house, besides. When he returns, the son of Hayato will be able to dress us all—all the inhabitants of Himari—in brocade."

Tomiko sat in one of the other rooms of the house and listened to the chatter of the tipsy guests. She sat alone in the dark and wept soundlessly. She had seen the son of Eda recently, down in the town, as he came driving up in a rickshaw and by chance stopped just where she was standing. He wore a snow-white shirt unbuttoned to the navel. His sleeves were rolled up above the elbows. The skin on Eda's chest and both arms were tracked with blue tattoos. As he jumped down from the rickshaw without noticing Tomiko, the carriage sprang up and the shaft scraped along the ground. Eda's son laughed roughly and threw a coin at the rickshaw man; repeatedly mumbling his thanks, the man picked it off the ground. Then Eda walked through the crowd of bystanders. Tomiko saw him glancing at several people, disparagingly appraising them with still, cold eyes.

Tomiko turned away quickly and lost herself in the crowd. Everywhere around her she heard the people whispering to each other how grand Eda was, returned from America dressed in brocade. But Tomiko trembled at the thought that this Eda could not have earned his many dollars in honest ways. That he must have moved through the big, unknown country on the other side of the Pacific with his eyes still and cold, like an animal in search of its prey. That was how he had won his countless dollars, she thought. And now that he had returned dressed in brocade, the people bowed to him.

Tomiko could not imagine that Nagayuki would also return dressed in brocade. Even if it were true, she told herself, that in America the streets are paved with gold, before he bent down to pick up even a single dollar, Nagayuki would ask ten passersby to whom the money rightfully belonged. Tomiko banished the idea of Nagayuki, his shoulders hunched like Eda, quickly reaching for the money that he had not earned by honest work. She knew how pure of heart Nagayuki was and how unable he was to change—even if the situation required it of him.

Tomiko could not possibly share her father's great expectations of Nagayuki. She worried that, once he was on his own in America, Nagayuki would be taken advantage of by people like Eda. I have to go with him, she thought again.

That was the main reason why, from the outset, Tomiko had been opposed to letting Nagayuki go to America alone. What was the purpose of such unnecessary haste, anyway? Surely Nagayuki could wait until the child was born and was old enough to be taken along. Tomiko was even prepared to leave the child in Himari, just as long as she could go with Nagayuki. She knew very well that he would need her in the New World. Even in Tokyo he had been helpless without her. He had said so himself often enough. That was why Tomiko did not understand why Nagayuki did not take her side and insist on going to America only with her or not at all.

The morning after that humid night under the mosquito nets, in which her father had announced his decision of sending Nagayuki to America, Tomiko had pleaded with Nagayuki not to submit to this decision. When she saw that Nagayuki hesitated and clearly did not know what to do, she did something that at the time seemed to her close to a lie; for she was not yet really certain that she was pregnant. Nevertheless, she told Nagayuki that she was carrying a child, hoping by her admission to alter the course of events.

Nagayuki hastened back to his father, to bring him the news.

"It has no bearing on your journey to America," Hayato said, unmoved.

When Nagayuki objected that the pregnancy had brought about a new situation and that Tomiko had spoken out bluntly against his going to America—at least at the present time, and alone—Father Hayato looked at Nagayuki silently and searchingly. Finally he lowered his head and closed his eyes for a moment. "I thought I had a samurai for a son," he said very deliberately.

When Nagayuki went back to Tomiko and had to confess that he had not succeeded in changing their father's mind, an overpowering rage engulfed her. For the first time she became painfully aware of what it meant to be married to a yōshi. A yōshi who was more obligated to her father than to her. Who submitted to her father. Tomiko asked herself if Nagayuki was quite unable to sense how hurt she was at his behavior. His eyes were trained only on her father. He admired him and wished to appear before him as a good son. By submitting to his will, he believed that he was acting properly. Father Hayato had the power to repudiate him anytime he was displeased with his yōshi. Of his own free will Nagayuki submitted to her father's will. Devotedly.

During these hours of impotent rage, Tomiko realized that Nagayuki was still the small, shy boy who had been adopted at the age of twelve, who since that time had been intent only on pleasing Father Hayato. The more clearly she realized this, the

38

more fervent grew her feelings for Nagayuki. Everything in her strove to protect him and to keep him from going into that alien, uncanny world on the other side of the Pacific. Over and over she considered every possibility of changing her father's mind.

Tomiko went to her father and recited all the reasonable arguments she could think of. She even shed tears before him, something she had never done before. For days she refused almost all nourishment, so that her mother was deeply worried about the baby Tomiko was carrying. "You must think of the child first of all," she said to her daughter.

Father Hayato patiently listened to everything Tomiko had to say. As he listened, he watched her, smiling indulgently, and explained to her in his calm, warm voice why Nagayuki must travel to America without delay and why this was the best thing for him and for the Hayato family. He explained to Tomiko that the great wealth Nagayuki would soon acquire in America was not important in itself, but only in relation to the invaluable experiences Nagayuki would gather in the Western world. He mentioned that in this way Nagayuki would contribute to elevating Japan's renown and would establish the name of Hayato far beyond the limits of Himari. Nor should it be forgotten, father said, that finally all the knowledge that had enabled Japan to rise during the past fifty years had come from the West. That was why Nagayuki must travel to the West; to see with his own eyes the people and the countries to which modern Japan owed so much.

Father's resolution remained unshakable. There was no question for him that Nagayuki must go to America as soon as possible. He was only waiting for the passport to arrive from Tokyo. As soon as it was in hand, Nagayuki would go to Kobe to obtain his visa to America.

"The best of our countrymen have traveled to the West, and there they have undergone immeasurably enriching experiences," he said, adding with conviction, "Nagayuki owes it to the name of Hayato to go, as well."

"All I want is to go with him," Tomiko said in a soft, pleading voice, "to help him to achieve what you expect of him."

"No samurai goes into battle with his wife clinging to his belt," Father Hayato explained patiently, gently stroking Tomiko's hair.

"But Nagayuki need postpone his trip only by a year," Tomiko began to plead once more. "By then our child will be born and will be old enough to be taken along. Nagayuki would also like to wait until then. I am certain of that."

For the first time, a trace of sternness marked Father Hayato's features. "Once a samurai has said yes face to face, he does not afterward say no."

"But it's not a matter of yes or no, just a postponement of the trip," Tomiko tried once more to protest.

At her words the sternness left her father's face, and he spoke lovingly to her. "As a good wife, you should not pull Nagayuki by the sleeve nor try to dissuade him with your tears from his courageous decision."

I'll even make a pile out of the whole business for your father. You know," he said, turning back to Father Hayato, "bankruptcy isn't a bad thing. Nowadays many shipbuilding firms fail because they lack a solid footing. But the main thing is to pull one's head out of the noose in time."

And he pulled his head down between his shoulder blades as if he were forced to loop a noose away from his neck. The skin across his massive nape formed two bulging folds. Except for a red line, they disappeared as soon as he raised his head once more. He winked meaningfully at Father Hayato and nodded to Tomiko with a friendly smile. His narrow, slightly swollen eyes twinkled in anticipation of his transaction.

Combined with his ripe Osaka accent, his external appearance and his quick, nimble gestures created the impression of an enormously agile businessman. Everything about him smelled of money, and Tomiko wondered why her father, who usually was unwilling even to talk about money, associated with this Sono from Osaka, with his undisguised interest in money and money alone.

All this time her father stood still, showing no emotion. He looked at the sky or at the trees cresting the steeply rising rocks at the back of the estate. Whenever Sono addressed him directly in his unbridled, bubbling voice, Father Hayato gave him a quick look and immediately turned back to more exalted matters. Only once did he nod distractedly; when Sono mentioned that he might even be able to extract a pile of money for him.

"Come," he interrupted Sono's flow of words, "I'll show you the hot springs at the back of the estate."

Tomiko understood that her father no longer desired her presence. The hint of financial problems which, as Tomiko could deduce from Sono's words, were the occasion of his visit, had disturbed her at first. That was why she took pains to observe this broker's face from the corners of her eyes. She could not, however, detect any malice in his features; only a very natural and probably pure pleasure in dealing with money.

5

When he saw the three men come through the gate, Father Hayato stepped outside the front door and stood under the carved crossbeam bearing the Hayato crest. Although it was an ordinary weekday, he was wearing his most magnificent Noh robe—a dazzling work of art of heavy rustling acid-green silk, in which undulating ornaments had been woven. The loose jacket he wore over it was a bright purple with twisting silver stripes and a pattern of flowers.

He had fastened his Noh mask in a most unusual manner to the back of his head, knotting the strap across his forehead. So he stood, a little threatening and hostile, at his front door.

Hayato stared impassively at the three men who, in single file, were crossing the steppingstones in the garden, coming ever closer to the house. The court official came first. His hesitant, groping steps made it quite clear how reluctantly he was undertaking the journey. Behind him, his two aides carried fat briefcases. Under the entrance portal, three steps down from the doorsill, the court officer came to a stop, made a deep bow, and allowed one of his assistants to hand him a scroll.

Before he could unroll it to read it aloud, Father Hayato descended the three steps from the sill without a word of greeting and walked past the official and his assistants into the garden.

The official bowed when Hayato stalked past him without looking at him. Then, embarrassed, he cleared his throat and handed the scroll back to his assistant. All three ceremoniously took off their shoes and entered the house.

Hayato walked along the house under the protection of the deep overhang, past the closed shojis, to the corner where the rock garden began. There he had placed his bonsai trees, and there he had for years spent at least half an hour a day. Some of the dwarf trees were older than he was. Others were ones he had begun to stunt when Tomiko was born. At regular intervals Hayato had clipped the trees, wound copper wire around their branches, and bent them in the desired position. That was how they acquired their aged, wind-driven appearance. Each spring he transplanted a few of them, in the process removing part of the root, to keep their growth down. The trees stood in flat stoneware bowls, and their roots wrapped themselves around stone fragments bedded in humus and sand.

The rock garden covered a circumscribed area beside the house. It was bounded on two sides by bamboo mats; the third side opened to the grounds. Beyond flat surfaces covered by mossy hummocks, the estate rose toward the hills in steps between azalea bushes, pines, and cedars. There, hidden among rocks and closely ranked trees, lay the hot springs that were considered the best and most bountiful in the region.

The rock garden beside the broad, sedate house, the family seat of the Hayatos for many generations, was laid out so that its irregularly curving forms reflected the sea and the soaring cliffs. The bonsai trees in it mirrored the pines that clung to the rocks of the steep coast with such unrelenting strength, withstanding the most violent storms.

Each day Father Hayato smoothed the gravelly soil with his bamboo rake and removed loose blades of grass, sprouting moss, and fallen leaves.

When Tomiko gave birth to her child, he had planted five new bonsai shoots. Every day he checked the leaf buds sprouting on the spindly stems, and in his mind he planned the unusual forms he would give the pliable young trees.

Michi was just three months old.

The softly vibrating, dying tones of koto music came from Tomiko's room. The baby slept.

The three men moved the small lacquered chest that stood beside the entrance to the large reception room away from the wall and pasted a slip to the metal door fittings in order not to damage the precious painted lacquer surface of the front and back as well as the sides. In the large reception room they removed the scroll from the tokonoma recess, rolled it up, and sealed it.

The men left no door unopened. Mother followed them silently on their way through the rooms. They walked through the house, and one of them wrote down whatever they saw. They examined the low dining table in the room next to the kitchen and affixed their seal to it.

In the dressing room, they opened every drawer of the kiri-wood wardrobe that reached almost to the ceiling. After they had convinced themselves that all the drawers contained silk kimonos, packed with enough little cloth bags of camphor to safeguard them against moths, they counted the kimonos and affixed a white paper strip from top to bottom across the drawers and pressed their red court stamp on it. Then they looked in all the closets, and if they contained anything that seemed worth confiscating, they wrote it down and sealed the closet doors.

The official opened the plain chest with the bronze fittings that stood in the hall to the innermost part of the house. He turned back the protective cloth and saw Hayato's Noh paraphenalia: the empty mask box, some fans, the manelike demon wig, and a sword lying on top of its scabbard. He closed the lid and told his assistants, who had already zealously begun to lick another official seal, that this chest must not be marked.

From the innermost part of the house, built of thick stone, where Father Hayato kept his stores of rice wine and all the lacquered utensils that could not tolerate sunlight and cracked easily in excessive heat, the assistants brought out more than sixty red-lacquered serving plates and pasted a seal on the inner edge of each. They placed seals on more than a hundred little lacquer bowls for soup and many tureens of various sizes.

When there were not sufficient stickers to stamp all the china bowls and all the wood and ivory chopstick containers, the court official had his assistants make a note of each utensil before putting them back in the storeroom. He sealed the door with particular care.

When he finally came to the servants' rooms and saw that these had already been emptied and abandoned, he wasted no further time there but went on to Tomiko's room, from which the softly plaintive music was still coming.

Surprised and annoyed, Tomiko interrupted her playing. She stared at the three strangers standing ill at ease in the doorway. Their heads were lowered, and they did not dare to raise their eyes. Tomiko was surprised to realize that her mother, equally ill at ease, stood behind the men without saying a word.

Several days earlier, when even the last servants who had lived in the Hayato mansion had gathered up their few belongings with tears and grumbling and had left the house, Tomiko sensed the danger hanging over it. As if anxious to defy the threat, on the evening before the official action of the court bailiff, her father had had dinner brought from a restaurant in town. For each of them—for himself, for mother, and for Tomiko—he had ordered eighteen different little bowls of the fanciest dishes.

The three of them sat in the small dining room they used daily and waited for the arrival of the runners from the restaurant.

On Father Hayato's face lay a strange serenity, such as Tomiko had never seen before. But her mother seemed restless and kept fiddling with her obi sash. The meal was brought on three serving tables; a taller one for the father and two lower ones for Tomiko and her mother. Father Hayato ordered the people from the restaurant to return the very same night to collect the tableware. Then, calmly and sensuously as always, he began to taste a little from this bowl and that. Tomiko was very hungry; nursing Michi had sapped her strength. So she devoured everything set before her, while her father took only half the dishes and left a little in every bowl.

"What do these men want?" Tomiko asked with annoyance. When the koto stopped, Michi became restless and began to whine. "What do they want? Why do they come in without asking permission?"

Her mother could think of nothing better to do than to apologize to the official for the improper and unnecessary questions of her daughter.

"Look after your baby." Her voice was bitter, and her eyes told Tomiko not to ask any more questions.

Tomiko picked up little Michi and stood in the room, irresolute. She watched as two of the men picked up her koto and put it back in its storage chest. They pasted a strip of paper diagonally across the opening slot and pressed the red seal over it.

"You can keep the baby things," the bailiff said to her. Turning to her mother, he added, "And everything else we did not seal." Then he mumbled some empty excuses under his breath and, bowing awkwardly, backed out of the room. His assistants also bowed and scurried away behind him.

When, as a final act, he had pasted another court seal on the doorpost of the entrance to the house, the official felt relieved because the whole embarrassing ritual had been completed. Quick, buoyant steps carried him around the house to the rock garden, where he intended to submit the long list to Hayato for his signature. As he turned the corner, he suddenly saw, sitting ahead of him on a block of stone, the figure of Hayato dressed in bright purple and acid green. An involuntary cry escaped him. Within the bordered square of the rock garden, Hayato's motionless figure seemed huge among the stunted bonsai trees. The Nōh mask was staring at the official with a dreadful expression, as if the seated figure were a spirit whose face was turned backward.

Slowly Father Hayato turned his head, presenting the bailiff simultaneously with his noble, previously invisible profile and the profile of the mask. With a motion of his hand, he invited the official to sit down. The court officer nodded uneasily and occupied another stone block next to Hayato. He brushed the crease in his narrow trousers and waited for Hayato to speak.

After a long pause, the words finally came. "When one looks passively, the primal language of life is experienced as silence. That bonsai tree over there"—Hayato spoke calmly, pointing his chin at a blossoming dwarf almond—"is as old as my daughter, Tomiko. Now the next generation has been born."

The court officer nodded, confused, and wondered whether to tell Hayato that of course the baby's things were not affected by the court decree.

"The I-captured spirit gradually sinks into the boundlessness of larger being. Reason is no longer necessary. Will falls silent. The heart has become still. The I has died."

The official murmured that he was sorry. "I took this step very reluctantly, and I only wanted to say—"

Hayato interrupted him, "What is essential is the objective silence that emanates from this spot. Do you see the old pine up there, high on the slope?"

The official, following his glance, nodded. "Yes. I can see it."

"Once it was struck by lightning, and for years I believed it would not recover. But it is green again. That is the fruit of inner maturity."

"It is good to see such a courageous tree," the official answered and slid around on his stone block as if he were getting ready to rise. "It is good. I have the list here. If I may be so bold. . . ." He forgot that he had meant to add that the dishes for daily use, all kitchen utensils, the stove, the mosquito netting, the bed linens, and two sleeping mats for each member of the family were exempted from the court order.

Father Hayato continued, "The destiny of each tree is unique and yet is repeated endlessly many thousands of times like lightning, which is the sword of heaven."

"Oh, yes, the Noh sword and the other stage equipment," said the official. "As far as I am concerned, these are inviolable family property."

He bowed to Hayato and spoke of his awe at the name of the old samurai stock.

"The most important thing about a bonsai tree," Hayato continued his thought, "is to crop the roots now and then when you prune the branches. Thus the trees will take on the expression of external and internal perfection."

Ill at ease, the official chewed his lower lip and clasped his knee with both hands. "That is important information," he got out and really meant to say that he would send a freight rickshaw to carry away the rest of the household goods because the house would have to be abandoned before the end of the day. That was the decision of the court, for which he was not responsible.

Hayato sat still, his knees spread wide so that the beauty of his rich silken gown was fully displayed. "Yes," he said. "For cedars, a soil mixture of thirty parts clay, forty parts sand, and another thirty parts humus is appropriate. But pines require a leaner soil—perhaps sixty parts sand and only ten parts native soil. Maple and all fruit-bearing deciduous trees need fifty parts of clay, twenty parts sand, and thirty parts humus. These mixtures give the best results."

His hand pointed to the dwarf pines and cedars which, under his shaping hand, had taken on bizarre forms, as if bent by storms or by constant ocean breezes. He pointed to the other trees, planted in bowls, where new green was sprouting. As he did so, the long sleeve of his purple-and-silver coat rustled along the stony ground.

"Don't be afraid to pick up the blooming almond tree," he said. "Today its scent is at its most pure."

After that, Father Hayato signed the inventory list without checking it over and cheerfully dismissed the court officer.

When the bailiff turned around once more at the corner of the house, to take his final leave with a respectful bow, the mask confronted him once more. A shudder ran through him, and involuntarily he leaned against the corner pillar of the house. Then he tore himself away. His quick steps led him from stone to stone down to the garden gate, his two assistants behind him. The sight of the mask pursued him. The empty eyes were fastened on him, and the sorrowfully distorted smile scorched his back.

6

Nagayuki's letters from America arrived irregularly and infrequently. He wrote that everything was even more overwhelming than he had imagined it would be. San Francisco was a beautiful city, built on many hills, and on the last hill near the harbor stood the telegraph tower, where signals were sent out whenever the fog spread over the bay and the ships could no longer find their way.

Many of the houses had been rebuilt since the great earthquake, of which the people still spoke with horror. Through the broad streets and up even the steepest hills iron carriages ran on tracks, their motive power supplied by steel cables laid under the ground. The weather had been cool and rainy all through the winter, and the people who lived here had told him that even in summer you could never count on truly warm weather in San Francisco. But barely twenty miles inland, even still level with the bay, the summer was so dry and hot that the water was crusted with salt, and it was possible to grow vegetables only by using artificial irrigation. The reason for this climate must be sought in the mountain chain which separated the inner, southern part of the bay from the ice-cold Pacific. In general, the landscape around San Francisco differed markedly from the region of Himari or anywhere in Japan. The coast was not as lovely, as sunny and divided into many inlets with steep cliffs; it was shallow and very foggy. In the interior of the country, however, right behind the protective chain of hills, desertlike stretches of land abutted directly on blooming gardens, and over to the east, in the far distance, one could see the snow-covered Sierras, the source of huge tree trunks which were felled by many Japanese workmen.

But most of the Japanese were employed in orchards and on farms. Some also worked on railroad construction, although the railroads were more likely to provide jobs for the Chinese. But many Japanese were engaged in the copper, silver, and gold mines in the Sierras and east of them. And although there was no real Japantown in San Francisco comparable to Chinatown, you could nevertheless buy anything in the city. Therefore, Tomiko need not worry about his health. He was well.

Father Hayato, who was reading aloud this most recent letter, as he always did, came to a stop. His features could not conceal his mood. In his very first letter, he had given Nagayuki to understand that the boy need not keep all the money until his return to Japan. Hayato had reminded him that the Yokohama Bank maintained a branch in San Francisco which he could use at any time to send any amount he wanted home to Himari.

Father had repeatedly inquired at the bank in Hamari whether any dollars had arrived for him. Always and again he had been told no. It seemed to Father that the bank officials' answers were tinged with ridicule, which offended him to the core. Everyone in Himari—also including the bank employees, of course—knew that Hayato no longer occupied his large old manor with many servants, but that he lived with only his wife,

Tomiko, and the baby in a single room in a shabby shed at the edge of town. There the strip of land between the latticed fence and the wall of the house was barely wide enough to hold his bonsai trees.

But Nagayuki knew nothing of the deep decline of the Hayatos, and Father had expressly forbidden Tomiko to send Nagayuki their new address. Therefore, Nagayuki's letters were addressed to the old house, the hereditary Hayato estate. The postman brought them to the shed at the edge of town.

In his last letter, Nagayuki had enclosed a photograph of himself in an elegant black suit and a stiff hat. Under his suit jacket he wore a white shirt with a high collar and a vest with a clearly visible watch chain. One hand, extended far from his body, held a cane with a curved handle; the other hand was poised on his hip. He had extended one foot, so that it was easy to notice his pointed, shiny shoes. He stood under the projecting trees of an avenue that led to a street hemmed in on both sides by tall buildings. In the background could be seen white people, tall and elegant. Some of them were holding dogs on leashes.

As if apologizing, Nagayuki had added at the end of the letter that until now he had had little opportunity to wear his kimonos. But he had carefully placed them in a warehouse for safekeeping. In every letter Nagayuki begged Tomiko to send him photographs of Michi. He had been very happy at the news that the birth had gone smoothly, and he always carried the first photographs of little Michi that she had sent.

Tomiko nodded and smiled to herself. She held the picture showing Nagayuki in San Francisco. He looked so alien in this photograph, and at the same time so proud, as she had always wished him to be. His eyes no longer seemed those of a yōshi; somehow they were different. She had never seen his eyes like this before. In the photograph, he stared at her with determination. For the first time since her disappointment, etched deep in her soul, that he had gone to America against her express wishes, she was attracted to him again. She felt rising in her a strong longing for Nagayuki, and she could hardly bear the warmth that filled her.

Later Tomiko said to her mother, "It would be wonderful if I could join Nagayuki in America."

Her mother, who had been ailing ever since the loss of the big house, replied, "But even more wonderful if Nagayuki were to come back soon with many dollars."

Tomiko looked tenderly at little Michi, who was just making her first attempts at grasping with her hands. Tomiko was certain that Nagayuki would be very attached to this child, even though she was only a girl.

Soon after that, a postcard arrived from Nagayuki announcing that he would be traveling in Alaska all summer. Father Hayato remained silent for three days. Then, full of bitterness, he spoke. "Nagayuki has clearly become a lordless samurai who does not know where he belongs. He travels through the land without a destination, and he has forgotten that he is a Hayato." Silent once more, he devoted hours to the care of his bonsai trees. He had already sold some of them to feed his family. A handsome bonsai tree fetched a sum sufficient for two months.

Without saying anything to Tomiko or her mother, Father Hayato visited the schoolhouse in Himari and inquired about the possibility of finding employment as a teacher. But the officials of the education department assured him that he was much too noble and highborn to take on such work. They could not possibly offer him a position as badly paid as that of a teacher. Father Hayato explained that it was simply to amuse himself and because at present he did not have much else to do that he wanted to teach calligraphy in a school, so that the young people might develop a sense of beauty. At that, the education officials expressed their regret; there were no openings to teach calligraphy in all of Himari.

In the single room where they all lived, Tomiko began to

spread out material, to cut it out, and to sew dresses in the Western style, as she had done in Tokyo while Nagayuki was studying at Todai and she had been bored in their big five-room house. She took the dresses to a small fabric store in town which was owned by one of her former school friends. But there was not yet any woman in Himari who might have worn something of the sort. All went dressed in cotton kimonos. Though many admired the Western dresses Tomiko had made, none was willing to buy them. So Tomiko took her designs back home, took them apart again, and turned them into children's dresses. These quickly found enthusiastic buyers. The demand grew so rapidly all over town that she had to sew more and more of them. In this way they were able to manage barely.

Nagayuki wrote from Alaska that he had now been in Sitka for two months. Here one could find salmon weighing as much as a hundred pounds, and sometimes the rivers in the interior were so full of the best fish that one need only stick a five-pronged wooden spear into the water to catch three or four at a time.

The next letter, in midsummer, came from San Diego, far to the south, near the Mexican border. It was the time of the apricot harvest, Nagayuki wrote. Sometime later he wrote from Santa Barbara, where the apricots were now ready for picking. Then came a letter from Fresno that also spoke of apricots. Here in the San Joaquin Valley was where he wanted to remain, Nagayuki wrote, until the figs ripened and perhaps until the grape harvest. He said not a word about the money he should have sent long ago.

Father Hayato maintained his usual silence and never mentioned money, or he alluded to it only with great circumspection. He continued to dress with the utmost care, as if the household still included several servants. Though he did not grumble when only six or eight dishes were put on the table—for he realized that Tomiko could not bring home four or five different kinds of fish from the market—as a rule he nevertheless expected to find about ten different bowls before him. Of these, in accordance with his traditional aristocratic habits, he took only small helpings, and left the rest. When her mother warmed up what he had left the day before, he scorned it, though he looked on tolerantly and without frowning when Tomiko and her mother ate it.

Father Hayato also continued to go into town regularly to meet with other friends of the Noh theater. Wherever he turned up, people rendered him almost the same deference he had enjoyed in the past, when he had still been the most distinguished citizen of Himari. He remained the living embodiment of the great family name. Such a name does not perish overnight.

Finally, on an early autumn day well over three-fourths of a year after Nagayuki's departure, a considerable amount of money arrived in Himari. Nagayuki had sent it to the local bank through the Yokohama Bank of San Francisco.

Shortly thereafter, the postman handed Father Hayato another letter from America. Nagayuki wrote that he could not return to Himari yet. He gave no further explanation for his decision to remain in America longer than had been planned. But Father Hayato who, as always, had read the letter out loud, said, "Nagayuki is doing well now. Everything points to a favorable trend. It's well for Nagayuki to remain an additional year and see to it that he will do even better. I shall practice patience."

Tomiko begged her father to give her the letter. Silently she read the whole letter once more from beginning to end and felt despair at the lines to which her father had paid scant attention during his reading: "It would be nice if Tomiko and the child could come here soon. That is why I am sending money. There is enough for a first-class ship's passage to San Francisco and a few travel preparations. Please tell Tomiko not to bring any kimonos. Here in America all the women wear Western clothing."

Screwing up her courage, Tomiko read the passage once more, loudly and clearly. When she finished, she gave her father and mother a questioning look.

Mother did not speak. As always, she deferred to Father Hayato's judgment. The state of her health had worsened during recent weeks. Only rarely and for short periods did she rise from her sleeping mat and sit at the table in their narrow room. She remained silent and looked at Father, wordlessly begging him not to allow Tomiko and the baby to leave.

Father Hayato pursed his lips and frowned in deep thought. Then a benevolent, pleasant smile again wreathed his features. He said, "Now Tomiko will no longer have to sew children's dresses for other people. We will buy a new koto, a few new bonsai trees, and much medicine for Mother. Run to the doctor this very evening," he added, turning to Tomiko. "Tell him to come."

7

The following morning, Father Hayato dressed with special care and went into town.

Tomiko, who was accompanying the doctor so that he could give her some more medicine, saw her father in conversation with the curio dealer. She knew that several of the objects from the old Hayato mansion had turned up in the shop of this dealer, especially the Sesshu scroll, which Father had once described as so precious as to be irreplaceable. It was over five hundred years old and came from the greatest painter working in watercolor. For some time, this scroll had been on exhibit, visible to all, at the entrance to the curiosity shop.

Tomiko felt a sharp stab when she had seen the scroll hanging there so totally without dignity, next to cheap woodcuts, feather tufts from Polynesia, silhouettes from Java, and other ill-assorted objects. Sesshu's gray falcon on the branch sketched by only a few brushstrokes looked quite lost amid the dusty pots, vases, andirons, teakettles, porcelain figurines, faded floor pillows, and shabby tables.

Tomiko had always hurried past this corner. Earlier, in the large reception room of their old house, the Sesshu scroll had captivated everyone who had entered the room. But here, among all the junk, it retained little of its old expressive power. The falcon on the steeply jutting branch seemed still to be resisting a strong wind. Its plumage, in washed tones of gray and black, stood out from the gray-and-white background, but his shadowlike, tightly clutching, flight-ready alertness seemed frozen.

Tomiko was surprised that the Sesshu scroll, which was supposed to be of such immeasurable worth, should hang at the doorpost of a Himari curiosity dealer, of all places. Perhaps, she thought, it is not an original after all but only a copy; otherwise it would have found a place in Tokyo or Osaka long since. There was no one in Himari who could afford a genuine Sesshu.

Tomiko saw that her father, head laid back, was examining the scroll. The dealer, rubbing his hands, stood beside him, incessantly bowing, his trunk springy and his knees soft. When Father entered the shop, the dealer eagerly pattered behind him. Tomiko hurried home to bring her mother her medicine.

That night, when Father returned, he radiated an air of satisfied cheerfulness. Until the small hours he sang and recited Noh texts he had not practiced for some time. The following morning and during the following days thereafter he devoted himself with renewed passion to Noh song and the evenings in communal practice with the town's other friends of Noh.

After six weeks he announced that, to commemorate the first anniversary of his son's departure for America and in gratitude for the news of his success he had received from there, he would produce a Noh performance in the Omiya shrine at his own expense. The Himari newspaper and placards all over town spread the news. Everyone remembered the fireworks of the previous year; the resplendent farewell to Hayato's yōshi, with the procession to the Omiya shrine and down to the harbor. The whole town was talking about the fact that surely Hayato must be very rich again.

Those who honored and admired Father Hayato fixed white paper bows to the holy sakaki branches in the Omiya shrine to reinforce his good fortune, and they intoned formulas of thankfulness before the altar. Those who envied him or who found his vanity unendurable prayed to the evil spirits that they might take Hayato's new riches from him.

Many spectators had gathered at the raised platform in the broad precincts of the Omiya shrine, where at other times the ritual Kagura dances were performed. The roofed-over stage, open to all four sides, had been festively prepared for the occasion. A ribbon of translucent purple material ran around the stage and was fastened to the four posts that supported the heavy, overhanging roof. Colorful tufts and white paper streamers were hung from the ribbon.

The decorations were so lavish because the Noh performance was dedicated to the gods worshiped at the Omiya shrine. For this reason all the dignitaries of Himari were assembled. Many other spectators had also come from the town and even from farther afield.

Altogether the program listed three Noh plays, performed, as the posters put it, by the "Himari Friends of Noh." Two comic interludes were scheduled between the serious Noh plays, for relaxation and laughter. These were performed by Kyogen actors, brought from the prefectural capital especially for this occasion. The performances lasted all afternoon.

Several hundred folding stools had been set up on the gravel-covered open space surrounding the stage, but they were not enough, and many spectators had to stand behind the last rows of seats. At the back there was constant coming and going, crowding and shoving, whispering and laughing, calling and waving between those who had already found seats and those who were still looking. Children ran across the gravel and called for their parents.

When the priest of the Omiya shrine opened the performance with a prayer, the sun was still high and enveloped the platform, under the overhanging roof, in cool shade.

The high point of the event was formed by the final Noh play because in it Father Hayato himself took the stage. By this time the sun had already sunk low and pushed the shadows from the square of the stage. It bathed the scene in a fiery light. The noise of the audience died at Hayato's entrance, and no one left his seat or gossiped with his neighbor.

The bright tone of the bamboo flute rang out pure and clear. With measured movements, Father Hayato crossed the stage, searching for his son, while the chorus's drawn-out, ceremonial songs declaimed the narrative. Father Hayato wore his acid-green gown with the dark-purple coat banded in silver, which he had salvaged from confiscation. In the light of the setting sun, the colors shone with an unearthly glow, while the accompanying text made the expression of his mask seem sorrowful.

Gliding along with seemingly weightless steps, hinting at the frailness of his old body, light as moldering, dry wood, the father wandered through an imaginary forest. The tapping of the little drum echoed like the beating of bamboo reeds against each other. The large drum droned dully, like distant thunder.

Then, when the son, searching for his father, made his entrance on the stage, the ground rumbled under his youthful steps. Though the son carried a heavy load of firewood which bent his back, he nevertheless stepped forth vigorously. The thumping of his steps was amplified by large stone urns which stood, invisible to the audience, below the stage. They served as resonators, and their booms mingled with the dull thud of the drums.

At the happy ending of the play, Hayato, in the role of the father, recited the closing words:

One who, like my son,
Restless, unresting,
With his own hands' doing
Cares for his aged father,
He is led by the gods
To the waterfall.
Water turns into wine,
And a single goblet
Of the gods' liquor
Cures sorrow and sickness,
Woe and weeping.

And everyone who attended the performance sensed that Father Hayato was speaking the words truly from his deepest, purest heart.

All were convinced that Hayato's yōshi would soon be returning, dressed in brocade, to rescue his father once and for all from his financial straits. Then Father Hayato would be able to move back into the large old house on the estate. Since the bankruptcy, the house had been standing empty because the new owners, a group of Tokyo bankers, evidently had no use for the property in Himari that had fallen into their hands. The storm windows had been put up and latched, and moss rooted on the roof.

The hot springs, too, the people in the town told each other, were gradually becoming overgrown with ferns. Some trees were said to have torn loose from the cliffs during the last typhoon and were lying in the water, moldering. At the shore of the pond behind the house, the front of reeds was advancing, and algae were about to displace the lotus blossoms on the surface of the water.

8

The autumn sky remained a deep and cloudless blue. As always, around this time of year, a cool wind blew in from the sea. The tangerines were ripe. Father Hayato sat by the mother's sleeping mat and peeled the freshly harvested fruits Tomiko had bought from the farm woman who daily trundled her two-wheeled cart along the bumpy road, calling out her wares. When Tomiko, the fiber basket on her arm, came to her, the farm woman bowed deeply, each time repeating that it was a shame to see Hayato's daughter in this very modest home. Since the farm woman had learned that Mother was ailing, she always laid a few extra fruits in Tomiko's basket and said that they were for the little miss. Michi was now old enough to crawl, and she brought much joy but also much work to the house.

Father often sat for hours on the doorsill and in his imagination brought to life over and over the pictures of his Noh performance in the Omiya shrine. Many people had told him that it had been a scene of almost unearthly beauty when he had stood on the stage. Everyone understood that the way he had danced and recited the role of the old father was at a level of perfection that could be achieved only by the spiritual power of a samurai whose family had cultivated sensibilities for the noble and the true for generations. No one else—not even another member of the amateur troupe—possessed the prerequisites for such perfect art.

People in the town congratulated Father Hayato for days— even weeks—after the performance. They expressed their hope that the echo of those wonderful hours would be carried on the winds across the Pacific, to the place where the honorable son of the house of Hayato was preparing his splendid return to Himari.

"As if all of life culminated in the expression of a single gesture," Father Hayato said, sitting at the doorsill, without turning his head toward the mother, who was lying in the room behind him. "You see?" he continued. "That is how it is in Noh. Everything is compressed into a single cry, which only makes the previous silence felt more strongly. You would have regained your health if you had heard this cry. Didn't you hear it? The gods were present at that instant."

The light's reflection lent a glow to the white strands which had increasingly begun to thread his previously jet-black hair. He joked about them, referring to them as "the snows of wisdom" that had fallen on his head.

"I could hear the applause all the way over here," Mother said. "Isn't that right, Tomiko? The applause could be heard all the way over here."

Tomiko was sewing. She sat on her old floor pillow on the tatami matting and had spread out a large piece of cloth in front of her. She was just attaching the sleeves to a child's dress. Michi was crawling back and forth between her and Father Hayato at the doorsill. She crowed with pleasure whenever Tomiko gave her a pat on the behind, well upholstered with diapers, as a sign that she should crawl back to Father Hayato. Each time Father stroked Michi's hair, and his index finger tenderly tapped her little nose.

Father Hayato was not entirely pleased that Tomiko was still taking homemade clothes into town for sale. But Tomiko refused any confrontation with him when, his voice unmistakably expressing displeasure, he ordered, "Put a stop to the sewing at last!" At those times Tomiko wordlessly put her needle aside and did other things in the house. But after an hour or so, she returned to her interrupted sewing. From her earnings for the children's dresses, she put a part aside, hidden. She did so with a bad conscience; never before had she had secrets from her father or mother. It would never have occurred to her to lay money aside for herself; especially not at a time when her mother needed medicine and there were payments to the doctor, who came with increasing frequency to check up on her. But Tomiko had been disturbed to see how freely her father had spent the money Nagayuki had sent. She wondered what possibilities she had for controlling his expenditures. As long as he took it for granted that any money was his own, her hands were tied. Nor was there any prospect that Father would change.

In certain ways Tomiko could not help but be pleased that Father did not complain about the loss of the family estate. Sometimes it almost seemed as if he were unaware of the change in his outward way of life. While everything around him sank into poverty, he remained unalterably the self-assured, proud samurai he had always been. For her mother it would have been an additional torment if her husband had filled the narrow four walls of the shabby room with self-pitying reproaches. Father Hayato never mentioned by so much as a word the evil of the people who had swindled him. Only now and then, when he awoke from hours of deep meditation, which he spent sitting upright before the disgracefully shabby tokonoma recess in the corner of the room, he said, "My heart is pure."

When he went to the simple chest with the bronze fittings and took from it the low music stand, placed the Noh texts on it, and began his recitation, an expression of inner peace illuminated his features. He lowered his voice so as not to disturb Mother or wake the sleeping Michi. Invariably he sat rigid, upright, his elbows spread far from his body, his palms pressed on his thighs, his legs crossed under him, in the same dignified position he had assumed on the stage. His lids were half-closed, and his eyes glanced only rarely at the page in front of him. He had long since committed all the texts and intonations to heart, and he turned the pages only as a matter of form. When he had succeeded in performing a particularly difficult passage to his satisfaction, he sometimes interrupted his recitation to say, with a transfigured smile, "Music cleanses the heart and assures me that never in my life have I acted wrongly."

Such statements proved to Tomiko that in his mind her father nevertheless wrestled with the loss of his property and was trying with all his might to overcome the bitterness that engulfed him. At such times she pitied him, and for his sake she was even glad that she had not yet joined Nagayuki in America. At the same time, she was bothered by the pity she felt, for Father Hayato's whole being was of the kind that tolerated no pity. He himself would have been the first to reject pity of any kind.

He retired into his Noh world. Removed from all lowly everyday life, Noh transformed human suffering into poetry. The power of the language, the dignity of the presentation, and the brilliance of the costumes steeped all that was ugly and unclean into beauty. The misery of a hermit close to starvation, the deadly fear of an inferior samurai were purified and raised to a level where they had nothing in common with the sorrows of this world. Father Hayato loved this form of poetry. Grief, in the form of lies and treachery, had descended on him and had brought him into poverty. But, inwardly, poverty did not touch him, for he was able to transform it into poetry. He lived in the certainty that the grief he had suffered had fitted him for the purest feeling.

This emotional certainty also marked his outward appearance and lent him dignity, even when he sat at the doorsill in his house kimono, which had already become quite threadbare, and looked up at the unchangeably blue autumn sky above the half-rotted latticed fence, over the roofs of the neighboring houses hunched low in their unpretentiousness. So Father Hayato sat on the worn doorsill and, in his soft, darkly sonorous voice, recited Noh texts.

When Tomiko's eyes ached from too much sewing and she could no longer clearly see the delicate thread, the strangely distant tone of his voice and the sight of his outlined figure transformed the narrow, light-filled door into a scene from the Noh theater. Sometimes it seemed to Tomiko as if her father's hair were already completely white, and this glow conferred even greater dignity on him. Soon he would be able to play the role of the old man on stage without a mask and without a wig, so shapely and wise did his face appear to her, and on his hair lay the snows of age. Tomiko could even hear the drums, the flute, and the crackle of the silken gowns.

Only the cranky voice of little Michi or her mother's cough as she lay on her mattress interrupted Tomiko's vision.

9

Against the pale yellow background of the wall, the Noh mask appeared supernaturally beautiful and terrifying. Father had taken it from the lacquered box whose sides could be unhinged once the lid was removed. For a moment, he stood irresolute in the room. Then he said to Tomiko, "This is the place for it."

At the designated point, Tomiko tapped a nail into the wall with a piece of wood. From that time on, the mask hung there and dominated the room.

Depending on the way the light was falling, the mask appeared vigorous or old and wasted. At night, when the light faded, the eyes glowed from their golden setting, and, in the increasing darkness, they remained visible as black holes. At such times the mask appeared awesome and had a demonic trace around the bitterly smiling, grief-etched lips. During the day, when the light fell full through the open shojis, this expression vanished again, making way for an enraptured beauty.

Tomiko did not like to look at the mask. She felt threatened by it. She would have preferred it if her father had left it in its box and had buried it deep in the chest with the bronze fittings. Her glance fell on the long vaulted chest, preciously lacquered in black. She remembered how unhappy she had been when her father, in spite of her express refusal, had bought her a new koto after all. The instrument was just as good as the one she used to own. The thirteen strings stretched over the long, arched sounding board remained untouched most of the time. The thirteen movable ivory pegs, used to tune the instrument, still wore the diaphanous layer of lacquer that the koto builder had applied to them to protect the finely polished surface. Only at her father's urging did she occasionally pluck the strings once or twice.

"The essential thing," her father said, "is to learn to free oneself from all cloudiness of the heart and to become as pure as a child."

Like a child who knows nothing about money or does not have to think about it, thought Tomiko, filled with bitterness—but I have to make sure that the money will not be wasted on something that postpones my trip to Nagayuki to an even more distant future.

"I cannot be as a child," she answered aloud. This made Father Hayato look up, amused, as if Tomiko's words were the expression of a fleeting mood, as if she were still a little girl. Then he would smile benevolently at her capricious whims and never say a word in reproof.

"Do you remember?" he asked, turning to Mother who, only half-awake, took part in the happenings in the room from her pallet. "Do you remember that our little Tomiko never wanted to be a child? She herself was still as little as a doll and nevertheless insisted that she was grown up."

"Yes." Mother laughed. "Tomiko was always like that. And now she has a child of her own already." Mother closed her eyes, and the expression around her mouth became careworn. "Too bad that it's a girl—as it happened to me with Tomiko. Our family will never bear a firstborn son and heir."

Father Hayato looked at her. "I never reproached you for not bearing a son. Tomiko is a good daughter, and Nagayuki a good yōshi."

Father rose to his feet and stood in the open doorway so that his figure darkened the room. "Nagayuki is quite all right," he said. "And when he returns dressed in brocade, I am certain a son will be born."

Tomiko examined her father's broad back and her mother's careworn face. She saw that Father's remark did not lessen her mother's grief, but instead increased it. She remembered the words her mother had spoken to her some time ago, the meaning of which had remained mysterious to her at first.

"It is only because of the son," her mother had hastily and softly whispered to her, as if she feared Father might hear; although he had left the house more than three hours before, and she knew very well that he would not return until late that night. Tomiko leaned down further to her mother in order to hear her. "Hang a cloth over the mask," Mother whispered. "I cannot bear its stare, and surely it is listening."

Tomiko took the dish towel and covered the mask. Then she returned to her mother's side.

"He goes there all the time and spends half the night with her. You know her—Rin. But it's not because of her but because of the son Rin bore him." Mother lowered her voice even further and continued breathlessly, hesitantly. "In the old days I didn't mind, for he is a strong, proud man. But the servant girls he kept taking into his room grew insolent toward me afterward. That is why I changed servants so often. Rin was different: better than the others, not insolent at all. You remember her. But when she became pregnant, I sent her away, too. We gave her a great deal of money at the time, so that the child could grow up properly. But unfortunately she had a son, and that hurt me very much."

The images thronged Tomiko's memory. Rin had been in their house a long time. Tomiko was deeply fond of her. Rin came from a family of fishermen with many children. She was untiringly industrious, always cheerful and conscientious. She was ten years older than Tomiko and considered it a great honor to be allowed to work in the Hayato household. Often she accompanied Tomiko to the hot spring that bubbled behind the Hayato mansion among the rocks. The hot water flowed down a row of moss-bordered basins that had been laid out generations ago by one of the Hayato ancestors. The water tumbled from one basin to the next, gradually cooling so that there was always one basin where the temperature was comfortable. An old pavilion with paper-stretched shojis around it stood at the edge of the largest basin among lush ferns and rampant trees. There was the scent of damp soil, of moss and mushrooms, mingled with a slight odor of sulfur rising from the water. Large stone slabs allowed them to regulate the strength of the flow.

As a child, Tomiko did not like the water to be so hot and therefore told Rin to lessen the flow. For Rin it was easy to move the heavy stone slabs—she was very strong. With one hand she could pick up the wooden pail full to the brim that stood on the stone platform in front of the pavilion and carefully and evenly empty the water over Tomiko's back. Rin had large, heavy breasts and a sturdy, strong body. She scrubbed Tomiko's back with a dampened loofah sponge, but when Tomiko said to her, "Come, Rin, I'll scrub your back now," she quickly crossed her arms over her breasts and said shyly, "The honorable young lady must not say such things. It is not proper."

Rin had long since faded from Tomiko's thoughts. Now, suddenly, she was back in her life. She wondered whether Father gave money to Rin when he visited her. She felt helplessly vulnerable. All she could do was silently hope that he gave Rin none of the money Nagayuki had sent. Since Mother had said that Rin had received much money at the time she was sent away, Tomiko reassured herself with the thought that Father probably did not make regular payments to Rin. She cautiously asked her mother, but Mother thought that Rin was not a bad woman and would surely not make any excessive financial demands on Father.

Tomiko watched her father's broad back, still standing in the doorway. She saw him slowly and with dignity descend the two steps that led to the narrow strip of soil between the latticed fence and the house wall. He was handling his bonsai trees. The metallic clatter of the shears revealed that he was cutting more branches off the dwarf trees to shape their growth to his will.

He forms everything to his will, Tomiko thought, and she felt hollowed out by unflagging, silent resistance. It seemed strange to her that her father was able to live so calmly. Doubt never seemed to enter him. He was always certain that what he did was right. He had very high standards for himself and would never have forgiven himself for failing. He always strove for the greatest perfection. The way he dressed, the way he walked through the garden or stepped through the front door, the way he stood before the shrine of the ancestors and cared for it daily, how he moved his hands, lowered his head—even his breathing—was free of haste and restlessness. He was so sure of himself that nothing of whatever happened around him disturbed his perfection. That was how he imposed his order on everything.

Tomiko knew that no words could pierce his shell of self-assurance. He let everything run off him like drops of water from a lotus leaf. Tears were foreign to him. The longer Tomiko thought about it, the more clearly she saw that to Hayato even Nagayuki was only another bonsai tree, which he shaped according to his will.

"I have written to Nagayuki," Father Hayato said at supper, "that under no circumstances can Tomiko go to America now, while Mother is so very ill."

 10

At night Tomiko often lay awake a long time. She listened to the familiar noises in the room. Father breathed deeply, and occasionally he snored softly. Her mother's breath was shallow and interrupted by coughing or drawn-out moans. Michi often crowed in her sleep and kicked her bare little legs. Tomiko had weaned Michi because after nursing she always felt so tired and also because her milk came only fitfully now that her days and nights were filled with restlessness and worry.

It took a month for a letter to get to San Francisco. And another month back. Tomiko had already written Nagayuki about Mother's illness and told him that she could not abandon her now.

So as not to worry him, she did not write that she had to run the house without help. She agreed with Father's comment that it would only burden Nagayuki to learn how much they had had to retrench. Nagayuki still believed that they were living in the

big old house, surrounded by servants and well taken care of. That was why her letter had mentioned no more than that Mother needed Tomiko's care during her illness.

Tomiko had made no mention of the fact that all the burden now lay on her shoulders and that every day she had to do the cooking for Father, Mother, and Michi. In the mornings she had to straighten up the room, wipe the tatami mats with a damp cloth, change Michi's diapers, put fresh water in the single little bowl of flowers in the improvised tokonoma recess, and prepare breakfast. She had to lift her mother out of bed and carry her to the toilet, she had to wash her and rub her skin with cream, had to adminster her medicine and feed her, just as she did Michi. Every day she had to wash Michi's diapers and hang them up to dry. Once a week she had to wash the whole family's laundry in a large wooden tub outside the door or, if the weather was bad, in the bathroom. Afterward her hands were quite raw, and her knuckles turned red from rubbing against the washboard until the blood seeped through the scraped-off skin. This was why she had stopped playing the koto.

But Nagayuki did not know that her old koto had been taken from her and that her father had bought her an expensive new koto with the money that had been meant for her to travel to America.

Nagayuki must not find out how badly things were going for her. Tomiko was quite sure that he was not wasting money on himself in America. Surely whatever he earned and had not sent to Himari he had put in the bank to earn a high rate of interest. Nagayuki would not speculate, sinking his money in risky investments. Before his departure Tomiko had impressed this caution upon him one final time, and he had made her a solemn promise. Nagayuki was keeping his promise; Tomiko was certain.

If he were to find out how badly off they were, his reaction was sure to be all wrong. He would certainly want to do without a servant himself—without a cook, if he found out that Father had had to dismiss his entire staff. He himself would eat only

cold rice, even do without hot water for his bath. He would not have his suits pressed regularly, and that would be bad for his reputation among the whites. He would go about in dusty shoes because he no longer wished to spend the money to get them polished, and he would stint on hair tonic. He would spend his evenings sitting at his desk and working, to earn even more money, just so that he could send it to Father.

When he had to travel, either to Alaska or to the south, he would go by third class and stay in cheap hotels. How easily he could be attacked by vermin there or become sick.

The idea that Nagayuki might become ill, so far away from her, in a strange country, threw Tomiko into sudden fear. She was firmly determined never to write him so much as a word about the fall of the Hayato family; for at the moment it was most important that Nagayuki further his career in America, unhampered by worry and fear. If she were to write him the truth about the way she and their parents were living, that she had to sew for other people just to keep the money he had sent from dwindling too quickly, he might even lose his head.

The worst that could happen now would be Nagayuki's precipitate return. He would be considered a failure in Himari; the whole town was expecting him to come back dressed in brocade.

But because he had refused the offers from Mitsui, from Sumitomi, from Toyo Textiles, and from the Yokohama Bank, he would never again be able to go to work for them.

Anyway, where could he go, Tomiko thought. Abruptly she realized that if Nagayuki were to return now without a considerable fortune in dollars, he could get at most a minor office job working for the city of Himari or a teaching position. The rest of his life would be haunted by the townspeople's whispers. Tattooed Eda and other such types would declare everywhere and mockingly: "Hayato's yōshi is a failure." That was why, in the darkness, Tomiko made up her mind. Whispering, she made herself the inviolable promise never to write Nagayuki

anything that might hinder his advancement in America.

Since she had weaned Michi and her breasts had almost entirely regained their previous shape and firmness, at night Tomiko often felt a pain, which she could relieve only by holding her breasts tightly. Then her skin remembered the touch of Nagayuki's hands. It was as if she were again feeling his playful hands, his fingers sliding along her throat, beginning to caress her breasts. Once again she felt his breath as he pressed down on her, pulling her to him in the many nights they had spent together in Tokyo—three years of nights.

In the beginning Nagayuki still showed the same shyness that had marked his behavior as the yōshi in the Hayato family from the day he had been taken in. Especially with Tomiko he had acted very insecure, ill at ease, awkward.

Tomiko remembered how it had been when Nagayuki joined the household. Both of them were still children. "Today the Ogasawara's son is coming," Mother said as she combed Tomiko's hair with special care, tying a large red bow in it.

Rin, who at that time served dinner every day, was told to lay two more floor pillows in the dining room, one to the right of Father and one across from Mother. "Why two?" Tomiko asked after Rin had left the room. "I thought only the new boy was coming."

"His mother is bringing him. She will eat with us."

"And the boy stays here?" Tomiko asked for the thirtieth time. "Stays here for good?"

"Yes. Starting tomorrow he is a Hayato, and later on you will marry him."

But for Tomiko at that time it was much more important that she would have someone with whom she could run through the grounds every day.

That evening at dinner she saw the new boy for the first time.

"This is Nagayuki," her father introduced him, "and Mrs. Ogasawara, his former mother."

Nagayuki, who was sitting in the highly honorable place to the right of Father, bowed awkwardly and so deeply that his forehead almost touched the tatami mat. He was very pale and kept his eyes lowered.

Nagayuki's mother possessed a strange attractiveness which captured Tomiko even then. Nagayuki's mother was quite different from her own mother. Her movements were flowing and very elegant. The way she bowed to Tomiko and then looked at her with a calm, self-assured gaze, probing and warm, made a lasting impression on Tomiko. Though Nagayuki's mother did not speak as she smiled and nodded at Tomiko in a friendly way, Tomiko sensed that this strange, fashionably dressed woman liked her, too. She wanted to ask her to stay a few days. She thought it would be nice to show the hot springs to this woman and perhaps to go into the steaming water with her. She would scrub her back with the loofah sponge and not have the feeling that there was something improper about it.

"Wouldn't you like your mother to be here with us?" Tomiko asked much later while bathing in the hot spring with Nagayuki. For an instant Nagayuki looked at Tomiko, quite lost. Then he turned his head aside and did not answer. It seemed to her for the rest of the day that Nagayuki was sad. He was once more cloaked in the timidity he had worn like armor when he first came to them.

At that time Tomiko did not yet know that, as a yōshi, Nagayuki was forbidden to think of his real mother. He had become a son of the house of Hayato, and no bridge could be allowed to exist between him and the Ogasawara family. When Tomiko began to understand the situation, because Father continued to weave appropriate admonitions into his conversations with Nagayuki, she also understood why Nagayuki was always so shy and sad.

Only at the hot springs, where they bathed daily, did he put off his timidity. Nagayuki was drawn there. Separated from the house and its brooding, oppressive size, away among the lush, flourishing trees whose arching branches almost brushed the water's surface, the stillness of the estate was accentuated by the rustling of the forest and the splashing of the water. There he sought Tomiko's company and spent many hours with her. He showed her the various plants growing along the watercourse, brought her insects and snails, explained to her everything he knew about these creatures, called her attention to bird calls she had never before heard so close by. In these familiar surroundings, Nagayuki put off his timidity with his clothes, and often as he stood at the edge of the basin, he moved proudly in the sensation of being almost a man.

Conversely, Tomiko became very shy when she was naked and jumped into the hot water ahead of him, although as a male he was owed precedence. Thus Tomiko became very familiar with the sight of Nagayuki's body. Only slowly and tentatively, during the years when her breasts began to round and the first body hair became visible on Nagayuki, did gentle desire grow in her to have him touch her. At the same time her shyness increased, and she was ashamed of being naked. She forced herself all the more to appear unself-conscious. When they bathed, she splashed Nagayuki from a safe distance or pelted him with moss she had scraped from the stones along the lip of the basin.

Now and again her parents also came to the hot spring. At such times Tomiko moved closer to her mother and Nagayuki to their father. So they sat still in the steaming hot water, moving only to wipe the perspiration from their foreheads. But once, when the two were alone and sitting side by side on the soft mossy pads at the edge of the basin, Nagayuki's hand touched the ends of her hair behind her ear, and slowly he slid his fingers downward while he pressed his body gently against her side.

Tomiko could still remember, as if it had happened only a few days ago, that a hot shudder had run through her body and she had nevertheless sat very still so she would not lose the feeling that engulfed her.

When Nagayuki touched her breasts, she leaned back and gave herself over entirely to the groping tenderness of his hand. Nagayuki never lost this groping, hesitant tenderness when he touched her body, even later, when they were married, and later

81

still, when he began to caress her body with his lips as well.

Tomiko thought of the letters which, as soon as she had begun them, she tore up rather than mail them to America. In these letters she was eager to tell Nagayuki of her longing. Time and again she realized that she lacked the words to express what she felt for him. The loneliness that sometimes overcame her like a sudden fever was strange to her as well. She could not get used to the loneliness; since she was ten years old, Nagayuki had always been with her. They had lived in the same house, called the same father Father, the same mother Mother, arose at the same time each morning, often walked together for a stretch of the way to school, ate together, played, quarreled, sometimes hurt each other through ambition or envy, for years could not quite imagine what they would do with each other once they were married.

Then came the wonderful time in Tokyo, where for three years they had lived only for one another. Looking back, Tomiko was sorry that she had often been discontented in Tokyo for no better reason than that her father would not let her study as well. Many hours had been wasted in talking about the courses she was not allowed to take. It would be nice to be holding a diploma now, Tomiko thought. She could be a teacher at her old school. That was a secure position, and even paid fairly well. Surely it was more interesting than sewing clothes for sale in the town. All the same, the three years in Tokyo had been wonderful. Nagayuki had been with her.

Now he was at an immeasurable distance. When she thought that a month would have to pass before he would hold her letter, and she would have no idea of his mood when he read it, she could not find the words to express her tenderness and longing for him. She dreamed that she was standing with him in the broad avenue she had seen in the photograph, wearing a beautiful Western gown with a broad-brimmed hat and high, pointed shoes. She imagined that, like a great white lady, she would walk through San Francisco arm in arm with Nagayuki, accompany him to his office, and at the entrance he would kiss her hand—a kiss that burned on her skin all day long.

She wondered what it would be like to sail to Alaska with Nagayuki or perhaps to travel on a large steamship. In Alaska she would see huge glaciers, all the way down to the ocean, and Nagayuki would catch a salmon for her—two feet long. Or he would take her with him to the south and show her places where thousands upon thousands of apricot trees bloomed. Tomiko dreamed that the whole world was scented with apricot blossoms.

II

One day Nagayuki's mother came into the fabric store in town just when Tomiko was delivering some more of her homemade children's dresses. Tomiko felt something close to fear when she saw Fumiya coming in the door; since Nagayuki's departure, she had not seen her again. But Fumiya smiled at Tomiko and did not seem surprised to meet her in this place. While they greeted each other cordially and bowed to each other—Tomiko, following custom, making each of her bows a little deeper—they exchanged only the usual inconsequential polite formulas, which expressed nothing personal. But Tomiko sensed at once that Fumiya had come expressly to meet her. She therefore hurried through her business with the shop owner so that she could speak with Fumiya alone.

"The townspeople are still talking about the Noh performance in the Omiya shrine. It seems to have been most sumptuously staged," Fumiya began.

Filled with bitterness, Tomiko bent her head. "With the money Nagayuki sent for my passage to America."

"How is Nagayuki?" Fumiya asked so quickly that her impatience became clear.

"He sent a photograph, and he seems to have made a place for himself," Tomiko replied almost cheerfully, adding, "too bad that I don't have the picture with me."

"I would like to hear everything about Nagayuki," Fumiya said, smiling tentatively.

"Hasn't he written to you yet?" Tomiko asked and realized at the same instant that her question was both foolish and tactless, for the news of a letter from Nagayuki to his real mother would have gotten around Himari quickly and would surely have reached the ears of Father Hayato. Nagayuki would never commit such a violation of the yōshi's obligation. Tomiko should have known as much.

Fumiya looked at Tomiko with a gentle smile and appeared eager to bury her sorrow. "I worry about Nagayuki," she said nevertheless, "and I'd like to have a longer talk with you sometime. Is there somewhere we can talk undisturbed?"

Tomiko noticed that the passersby were casting curious glances at her and Fumiya. Some bowed in greeting, and she returned the gesture. Fumiya, too, was constantly greeted by passersby. Everyone in Himari knew the Lady Ogasawara, whose tempestuous fate had for a long time furnished the town's chief topic of conversation. The townspeople offered Fumiya their shy admiration, for Fumiya was the symbol of the old Ogasawara dynasty, which for many centuries had played a crucial role at the imperial court in Kyoto.

"We can't stay here any longer," Tomiko said with an expression of regret. "Everyone is looking at us with so much curiosity."

Fumiya added, "Tomorrow the whole town will know that we stood on a street corner and talked. Everyone will even claim to know what we talked about."

"We could meet tomorrow behind our old house, on the top

of the cliff," Tomiko suggested. "The way up there is steep, but we will be undisturbed."

Before parting, Fumiya asked, "If it would not be too much trouble, do you think you could bring Michi? I would so much like to see her."

"She resembles Nagayuki a great deal," Tomiko said. "She has the same oval face and the same pale skin, like porcelain."

Fumiya took her leave very formally, with a series of bows. Perhaps she spoke the usual polite phrases a little more loudly than necessary because she felt the curious stares encircling her and Tomiko from all sides.

Tomiko stood still a moment longer, watching Fumiya as she walked down the street toward the southwestern rice paddies. At their edge, outside the town limits, stood the old estate manager's house to which the Ogasawaras had retired after they had been unable to wrest their Kyoto property from the confusion following the Meiji restoration.

Tomiko knew that Fumiya occupied a special position within the Ogasawara clan. Her childhood had coincided with the time when the imperial court was still in Kyoto and the Ogasawaras determined the life-style at court through the ceremonial office which they had held uninterruptedly for more than six centuries. Fumiya had grown up in this sheltered environment, where the days were arranged according to highly regimented rituals. Every day was predetermined and filled with activities intended to approximate the course of nature in constantly new and yet infinitely repetitive rhythms.

Spring, summer, autumn, and winter, as well as the transitional seasons in between them, were echoed in the poems that were recited from ancient sources or newly composed according to strict formal laws and verbal associations. To these were added ritual actions before the Shinto shrines and in the Buddhist temples all through the city as well as occasional performances of Bugaku dances—handed down unchanged for far more than a thousand years—and listening to old courtly music. As far back as Fumiya could remember, life ran its course between blossoming cherry trees and maples resplendent in autumnal, fiery colors. One whole summer night was taken up with the light dance of glowworms, and one night in early autumn was devoted to a celebration of contemplating the moon.

Fumiya had grown up in this world of seclusion and artificial peace. The refinement of social manners and the exquisite extravagance of taste that prevailed at court influenced her early years. But when, with the fall of the Tokugawa shogunate, the times changed and the Tenno was transplanted to Tokyo, there to serve as the symbol of power to the era of the new Japan, the old court nobility in Kyoto fell into insignificance. While in Tokyo the Tenno grew into a figure of political-military strength, life at the court of Kyoto lost all importance and status.

During this period of decline, Fumiya broke out of the circumscribed world of the imperial court, which had become senseless. Against the wishes of the entire Ogasawara family, she married a young engineer who was neither a nobleman nor a samurai. Fumiya moved to Tokyo with him and lived there for thirteen years. During this time she gave birth to three sons, of whom Nagayuki was the youngest. Through her husband—who was considered one of the ablest bridge builders of the new Japan and was even once sent by the government on a study trip to America—Fumiya met many white scientists and advisers who had come to Japan from Europe and America.

But then Fumiya's husband died in the collapse of a bridge. Fumiya and her three sons returned to the circle of the Ogasawara family, who in the meantime had retired to Himari, to the home of their onetime estate manager.

Tomiko knew how difficult it had been for Fumiya to satisfy the requirements of the Ogasawara clan for her readmission into the family circle. It had been demanded of her that she give away her youngest son, Nagayuki, as a yōshi, for the Ogasawaras were very numerous themselves and had great difficulty living on what they still owned in the way of land and other possessions. Fumiya fought for five years to keep Nagayuki. But she knew that she would be unable to pay for his schooling after the age of twelve. Then they heard that Hayato was looking for a yōshi, and the Ogasawara clan decided that this was a favorable opportunity to dispose of Nagayuki.

Barely three years later, the Russo-Japanese War broke out, and both of Nagayuki's brothers died in battle on the same day, outside Port Arthur. This happened before Tomiko's marriage to Nagayuki.

Thinking back, it occurred to Tomiko that this event must surely have worried her father considerably. Suddenly she also understood the great touchiness he always showed if he heard so much as a mention of the name of Ogasawara. He was plagued by fear that Fumiya would come to claim her youngest son. For a while there was even a rumor in the town that Hayato's yōshi would be returned to the Ogasawaras.

Fumiya heard the rumor, too. She was therefore extremely reserved in all her encounters with Father Hayato and Nagayuki. She avoided any meeting; her feelings told her that Nagayuki had joined Father Hayato as his son, with all the power of his loyalty. Tearing him away from this attachment, which had been formed so recently, would surely have uprooted him completely. Fumiya did not want this to happen. Suddenly Tomiko realized what an enormous sacrifice it was for Fumiya to have given away her youngest son at the age of twelve, never again to be allowed to think of or speak to him as her son, though they lived in the same town.

Lost in thought, Tomiko walked down the street and turned into the narrow alley that led to the seedy quarter, to the house where all of them lived in a single room. The thought that Michi needed her quickened her steps, and she ran the last hundred yards to get to her child quickly and hold the little kicking bundle of life in her arms.

"I'm glad you're back," Mother said softly from her mattress, smiling gratefully at Tomiko.

"Where is Michi?" Tomiko asked.

"With Father." Mother gestured vaguely.

Tomiko wondered whether to tell her mother that she had

run into Fumiya, but then she kept silent about the meeting in town although Mother had never indicated any dislike of Fumiya. Tomiko did not want to add another burden to her mother's anxious thoughts; the mention of Fumiya's name would have awakened memories of former times, when the Hayatos were still living in wealth and Fumiya, when she came to see Nagayuki, had to use the servants' entrance to demonstrate to all the world that she no longer had any claim to Nagayuki. After her other sons had died at Port Arthur and rumors coursed through the town that Hayato's yōshi would be returned to the Ogasawaras, Fumiya completely ceased her occasional visits to the Hayato house. She had not returned until the wedding; only at the special insistence of Father Hayato had she assumed a place of honor.

The time between the wedding and the move to Tokyo for Nagayuki's education passed quickly. It was not until Fumiya came to Tokyo to visit Nagayuki and Tomiko that Tomiko realized that her relationship with Fumiya was really quite unusual. Generally there is a silent battle between a man's mother and her daughter-in-law. Each one tries—one as a mother, the other as a wife—to gain greater influence behind a façade of feigned cordiality. Tomiko abhorred this sort of false intimacy which, as an outsider, she observed among her married friends in Himari. In Tokyo, too, where she made new acquaintances, she noticed how deep ran the enmity between most of the young women and their mothers-in-law, although outwardly great value was placed on cordiality.

It was different with Fumiya. She laid no claim to sole possession of Nagayuki's affection but tried to strengthen in him the feeling that his relationship with Tomiko was the best and most wonderful thing she could imagine for him. From this Tomiko concluded that Fumiya had a special liking for her. When Fumiya very openly asked her, in her quite inimitable manner—a mixture of cordiality and polish—to put aside the usual formalities that regulated the relations between a young woman and her mother-in-law, Tomiko agreed joyfully. She herself had already begun to think of Fumiya as an older friend.

Fumiya had last come to the Hayato mansion at the time of Nagayuki's departure. There was a heated discussion between her and Father Hayato, who had irrevocably determined Nagayuki's journey to America. Since then Fumiya avoided encounters even with Tomiko. Therefore, Tomiko felt a certain relief to have seen Fumiya again at last. She knew that Fumiya had deliberately brought about the meeting, and she looked forward eagerly to the next day. She would be glad to carry Michi up the steep path to the top of the cliff where she had stood that day, her eyes filled with tears, watching the procession carrying Nagayuki to the Omiya shrine and then down to the harbor.

In her mind's eye she could still see the moving throng. Her father leading the way. Nagayuki at his side. Then the five high-piled rickshaws, trailed by the rows of other guests, led by her mother. On both sides of the road were the crowds of spectators, their jubilation sounding like derisive laughter. The wind carried the sound up to Tomiko. Mingled with the jubilation was the drawn-out cry of the sea eagle who was gliding along the coastline on the updraft, watching for prey.

12

When the automobile stopped on the bumpy street in front of
the little house, it was a sensation for Himari. A large crowd of
children had run alongside the car, shouting and shrieking,
from the town center out to the modest shack. Everyone wanted
to see and touch the noisy monster that moved by itself, without
visible outward means.

The people of Himari had read in their newspaper that there
were already forty automobiles in Tokyo. Eda—the brocade-
clad son of the dockworker Eda, returned from America, as the
people spoke of him—had also told them about the automobiles
that were already such a common sight in the streets of San
Francisco that no one bothered to turn his head after them
anymore. But in Himari it caused a sensation when such a
symbol of progress drove through the streets of the town.

Everyone expected the automobile to stop in front of the
mayor's house, and they tried to catch a glimpse of the figure in

the back seat. But when the chauffeur stopped someone on the main street to ask him the way to Hayato's house, the news spread that Hayato's yōshi had returned from America, dressed in brocade. Only those who had seen the automobile from up close said that the man in the back seat was not Hayato's yōshi.

Tomiko looked up from her sewing as the noise in the street came closer. "What can that be?" she asked her mother.

A short time later, the noise stopped right in front of the house, and only the children's voices could be heard. "This is where Hayato lives," they shouted.

Then Sono's round red face appeared in the door opening. "Excuse me. Am I disturbing you?" he called in his unmistakable Osaka accent.

"Oh, Mr. Sono," Tomiko replied, laying aside her sewing. "Father Hayato is not here. Would you like to come in anyway?"

Sono brushed the dust from his clothing. "A long trip," he remarked, laughing loudly. "It blows right through you." Then he clumsily undid the laces of his Western shoes, pulled the shoes off, and finally entered. When he saw Mother resting on her mattress in one corner of the room, he came to a halt, hesitated for an instant, then went to her with quick steps, his head bent low. He sat down near her pillow and bowed all the way to the tatami mats, in spite of his corpulence, so that he almost split the seat of his trousers. "I am so very sorry not to find you in better health."

He looked at Mother sadly, then gave her an encouraging smile. "It will all be well again. Life is like that. Sometime or other things start to look up. That business about the bankruptcy—I was so sorry about that, too. I tried everything in my power to steer the bankruptcy in a favorable direction. But you know I am only a broker, unfortunately, and not a magician."

He laughed at his own words and repeated, "Yes, magic is what my profession needs. Here in Himari the name of Hayato is a word to conjure with. Such an honorable name, so old. It opens doors and hearts here in Himari. With the backing of such a name, all deals run smoothly," Sono called out cheerfully, clapping his ankles. "With the glow of an old name, one can bring off favorable deals even at the gates of hell." Sono smiled broadly and added cunningly, "That's what we businessmen in Osaka say. But this time hell was in Osaka, and the glow of the Hayato name was shrouded in dark clouds. Unfortunately, that was why the bankruptcy business ran its course differently from what I had hoped."

Again his face looked distressed, and he massaged his knuckles.

Mother smiled in reply. When she spoke, her voice was low. "I thank you for your concern. I am sorry that my husband is not at home."

"It doesn't matter," Sono immediately called, in a voice that had regained its cheerfulness. "Actually—" He stopped and turned to Tomiko, who had been preparing tea and was offering it on a small tray. "Actually . . . I just wanted to try out my new automobile. You know, until now there have been only four automobiles in Osaka, and I have just now acquired the fifth. Since I visited you last," he continued stroking his scalp in embarrassment, "you know, I hardly know where to look . . . I mean, since I first met the beautiful daughter of the Hayato family, I have been firmly resolved that my first long trip in my new automobile would lead me here, to Himari."

He wiped the shyness from his forehead and looked at Tomiko ingenuously and boldly. "That's how it is." He nodded, adding, "And now my eyes can't get enough of the beauty that fills this room with brightness."

"Oh, come," Tomiko replied, not a little embarrassed. She was unsure whether to be amused or offended. But when she saw how honest the smile on Sono's face was, she decided not to take offense at his unsuitable bluntness. She was not even insulted by the fact that he looked at her with a mixture of wonderment and undisguised cupidity, for his glances bounced off her.

Tomiko was about to say that she must rush off to find her

father, who had taken Michi for a walk, when Sono jumped up like a rubber ball and called, "I've brought a present!"

He rushed to the door and in a thunderous voice shouted to his chauffeur to bring in the package. It was a huge carton that the chauffeur put down on the door sill. Sono began to unpack it. "Actually, this isn't proper," he chatted, laughing as he spoke, "to unpack one's own present. But I'll make an exception this time because I have to show you how the thing works."

Several curious children, who were still standing around the automobile in dense clusters, stuck their heads in the door. They wanted to see what was inside the big gift box. While Sono removed the thick cord and all the packing paper, he asked Tomiko if she would do him the honor of allowing him to invite her for a drive in his automobile.

"No," Tomiko replied. "When Father returns, I will have to take care of my child."

At that, Sono's hands stopped in the tangle of twine. "Oh, yes," he said, disturbed. "A child. . . . The beautiful daughter has a child."

"Of course," Tomiko laughed at him, "a nine-month-old daughter."

Sono shook his head in disbelief and, seeking help, looked at Mother. "But last time she wasn't even married. She is Hayato's daughter, isn't she?"

"Yes," Mother nodded. "Tomiko is our daughter, and her husband is in America."

Weary, Sono sat down on the bare tatami mats to order his thoughts. "As best I heard, the only son of Hayato is in America. That must be the brother of the beautiful daughter, then, not her husband."

At that both of them laughed out loud, Mother and Tomiko. "Our son is a yōshi," Mother explained.

"And for that reason my husband," Tomiko added.

Confused and slightly less enthusiastic than before, Sono continued unwrapping his present. Finally he unveiled a flat, square wooden chest, bordered and carved, with a large movable rubber disk on top.

"This is a gramophone," he announced proudly, placing a shiny, chiseled metal funnel on it. "You can use it to make music." His extended fingertips extracted a black disk from a paper bag. "This is a record," he said, nodding at Tomiko, and asked her to come closer so that he could demonstrate the mechanism to her.

While Sono was turning the hand crank to wind the spring, Father Hayato returned, carrying Michi.

13

The smell of Sono's cigar smoke still clung to the walls and had seeped into the tatami mats. Mother coughed more than usual. Michi crawled around the gramophone and kept grabbing the shiny metal funnel from which the shrieking music had blared.

Father did not dignify the presence of the gramophone with so much as a glance. Tomiko picked up the instrument and, without much ado, took it to the storage chamber. Michi, who had begun to pout when Tomiko put away the gramophone, began to cry piercingly, so that Tomiko picked her up quickly and promised to fold animal figures for her out of paper.

Tomiko cut the wrapping paper Sono had left behind into many squares of various sizes and spread them out on the tatami mats. While Michi scribbled thick lines on the paper with a pencil, Tomiko folded one after the other into a fish, a water buffalo, a horse, a cat, and a dog and set them up in front of Michi.

Michi wriggled with joy and would not give up until Tomiko had also folded cranes. When all the animals were done, Tomiko had only to point to each figure with her finger, and Michi said bow-wow, meow, moo, clop-clop, or moved her arms like fins in the water or wings on the wind.

Father Hayato pushed his floor pillow to the corner of the room, the place where Tomiko generally unrolled his mattress each night, and began to take his tea-ceremony utensils from their protective cotton wrappings. He unpacked each piece, wiped off the dust, and set them carefully before him in precise order. Tomiko had to hurry to prepare hot water.

Whenever he had something on his mind, Father was especially exacting about the tea rules. He prepared his tea with exquisite deliberation and drew out the ceremony until time seemed to stand still.

Tomiko watched the solitary tea ceremony with only half her mind. Michi, happy with her origami figures, had quite forgotten the gramophone. Father Hayato performed the gestures and prescribed actions with the utmost precision. He lost himself completely in the tea ceremony. He seemed quite unaware that he had to carry it out in a corner, hemmed in by household effects and objects of daily life.

"The tea hour is the time of pure experience," he used to say, "when the essential eclipses the shabbiness of everyday thoughts and worries."

That was how it had been, he himself had pointed out several times, when Fumiya had visited him to beg him not to send Nagayuki to America. They had still lived in the old house. Father had received Fumiya in the tea chamber, where he customarily invited only those visitors to whom he wished to accord special honor. The tea chamber was in a small extension next to the rock garden, where the bonsai trees stood among miniature rocks, gravel, and mossy banks. The tea chamber could be entered only by a very low door. Except for a scroll in the tokonoma recess and a flower arrangement before it, the room was quite bare. On that day Father had removed the usual scroll from the tokonoma recess and hung the impressive falcon by Sesshu there instead. He had asked Tomiko to fill the vase with flowers.

Tomiko had secretly listened to the conversation from the next room. At first she had heard only the sounds indicating that Father was putting the powdered tea in the drinking bowl, then pouring a ladleful of hot water over it, and finally beating the tea into a foam. A soft, scraping noise announced to Tomiko that Father Hayato had placed the tea bowl in front of Fumiya and that she, after the usual measured bow, had picked it up.

After the proper silence, Fumiya, as expected, praised the deliciousness of the tea and the beauty of the bowl. She praised the balanced irregularity of form, the dull glow of the cracked glaze, and its warm gray-white color, which contrasted pleasantly with the bright-green foam of the tea and the dark-green brew.

"It is only a Shino bowl," Father admitted.

"Oh!" Fumiya dutifully breathed. "A particularly precious piece."

"A family heirloom," Father explained. "Originally a gift from the shogun to one of my ancestors."

For a long time Tomiko heard nothing from the next room except the soft rustle of silk. Then Fumiya said, "I have heard that Nagayuki is to be sent to America."

Father Hayato seemed to have been waiting for these words, and immediately he began proudly to tell what kimonos he had ordered expressly for the journey. The choice of materials in Himari had been too modest. That was why he had sent for kimono dealers from the prefectural capital to come to Himari, to select for Nagayuki the most beautiful kimonos ever seen in America.

"I also chose the best lining materials for Nagayuki's kimonos, all of the most delicate silk, hand-woven, so he can go anywhere and be respected by all," Father continued. "No one shall be able to say of Hayato's son that he is not nobly clad."

"But in America?" Fumiya's soft voice questioned. "In America kimonos are not worn, especially not by men."

"True beauty finds its admirers everywhere," Father Hayato replied coolly, "and everywhere there are four seasons whose essence is caught in the patterns, textures, and colors of handsome kimonos. I chose Nagayuki's kimonos with this thought in mind. They will not fail in their effect even in America."

"That may be," Fumiya said, and Tomiko sensed from the sound of her voice how hard she was trying to suppress her agitation.

"When he walks out in the streets of San Francisco dressed in such kimonos, all the people will step aside respectfully and bow their heads to his beauty," Father continued. "Everyone will wonder who this proud samurai is, striding through the streets."

"When my late husband was in America over twenty years ago," Fumiya began quietly, "kimonos aroused no nods of approval but only head shaking, and anyone who wore a kimono in the street was roundly laughed at. I assume that it is no different today than it was twenty years ago."

"Twenty years ago Japan was not yet a great nation. Since then we have defeated Russia and annexed Korea. Taiwan belongs to us, and our imperial troops are on the soil of China," Father replied in a superior voice.

Tomiko sensed that the mention of Japan's military involvements could only tear the scab off Fumiya's memory of the death of her two other sons. She realized abruptly that Fumiya had been driven by the courage of desperation to make this visit to Father Hayato; for it was not proper for her—Nagayuki's mother—to push herself into the relationship between Father Hayato and his yōshi. Rather, Father Hayato expected Fumiya to feel pride and gratitude because he was sending her former son to America. But Fumiya did not conceal her fear that Nagayuki's projected journey could end quite differently from Father Hayato's expectations.

Tomiko would have loved to shove the sliding door aside and throw herself on the ground before her father to beseech him together with Fumiya not to send Nagayuki away.

"When my husband was in America," Fumiya began again, "he saw how the Chinese were oppressed in building the railroad. Even the white men admitted that every railroad tie covered the grave of a Chinese workman. In San Francisco my husband saw for himself how Chinese men, women, and even children were lynched by white crowds—"

"Fortunately, a Chinese coolie and a Japanese samurai have nothing in common," Father Hayato interrupted her. "Such events do not affect Nagayuki."

"Americans do not distinguish between Chinese and Japanese. For them, the world contains only white, yellow, red, and black, and they look down with contempt on anyone who is not white. My husband was almost lynched himself—he would have been lynched if the American engineer who had been assigned to him to inspect modern bridge constructions with him had not saved him—"

"Because he was Japanese," Father Hayato determined with unshakable matter-of-factness.

"No." Fumiya was almost shouting with anger. "Because, as a member of the yellow race, one is unprotected in America unless one is shielded by a strong protector. One must be allied with a large Japanese concern or have been sent directly by our government. Then one can enjoy safety. Only then."

"I have trained Nagayuki to be a samurai," Father corrected Fumiya without altering the cordial tone of his voice. "A samurai is always strongest alone."

The silence that followed weighed on Tomiko almost more heavily than her father's words. Tomiko felt as though Fumiya's trembling agitation were seeping through the paper-covered wall separating her listening post from the tea chamber. For a time nothing could be heard but the rustle of silk and the bubbling of the tea water which was still softly and steadily steeping in the iron kettle.

"May I prepare another bowl of tea?" Father asked, and Fumiya replied haltingly, "No, thank you."

Tomiko heard her father beating foamy tea for himself without undue haste. "It is beauty which opens hearts and puts people in a frame of mind that makes them receptive to the true values of life. Then people realize what is genuinely beautiful and always remains beautiful—unchangeable through the centuries," her father said reflectively. "That is why for Nagayuki's kimonos I chose patterns the beauty of which was already acknowledged in the early Edo period."

Fumiya spoke again. "To the best of my knowledge, Americans are very prosaic people, little influenced by the delicate beauty we value here in Japan."

"Nevertheless, Americans are very clever people," Father Hayato replied as he calmly continued to whip his tea into foam. "They are clever and they are rich. One hears it again and again. They will not pass up the opportunity to gauge Nagayuki's worth adequately."

"Americans have quite different ideas of worth than we do," Fumiya contradicted with gentle patience.

"When Nagayuki walks through the streets of San Francisco," Father Hayato described what he already saw in his mind's eye, "people will stop and turn to him to learn from Nagayuki's lips about life in Japan."

"And then?" Fumiya drawled.

"At the beginning is always admiration. It will be given to Nagayuki in rich measure once he is in America."

"He cannot live on admiration."

For the first time a scornful undertone crept into Father Hayato's voice as he replied, "Of course admiration is followed by many invitations, and these are combined with valuable gifts. After a short time, the cleverest of the Americans will wish to use Nagayuki as an adviser in questions concerning the law and, of course, also in all questions concerning good taste, style, and beauty. In this way they will soon dress Nagayuki in brocade."

"I doubt that these hopes will be fulfilled," Fumiya said politely but very firmly.

At that, Father Hayato laughed. "But Nagayuki was the first in his class when he graduated from Todai. They will realize very soon in America how great his knowledge is and that he comes from the very best family. That is why Nagayuki should rent a large house in San Francisco, where he can invite his guests and entertain them. I am giving him three double sacks of rice from our own fields, the best uji tea, and. . . ." Father's voice stopped. He was silent for a moment, as if a new, important thought had struck him. "Nagayuki shall even take this Shino bowl to America, which in its cracked glaze bears the brilliance and dignity of many centuries. When the governor of California visits him in his home and he can place this Shino bowl before him, the impression will be overwhelming."

The rivers are full of them. It must have been an interesting adventure for Nagayuki."

Fumiya looked at Tomiko searchingly. Then she spoke slowly, as if unable to trust her own words. "Don't you know that Sitka is the place where there is nothing except a couple of large canning factories?"

"You mean he is involved with a fish cannery?" Tomiko asked, incredulous. "A Todai graduate?"

"What else could have kept him in Sitka for three months? They use many Japanese there for canning salmon."

"But Nagayuki is a Todai graduate. He doesn't need to do such menial work. Whatever you're thinking—you must be wrong. If what you say is true, that there's nothing but fish canneries in Sitka, then I think it is much more likely that Nagayuki was there as a legal adviser. Probably a prominent factory owner from San Francisco sent him."

"I doubt that Americans have ever heard of Todai, and even if they have, and if they know what it means for someone to have studied at the first imperial university of Japan, it is still doubtful whether there is any need for the skills of a Todai graduate like Nagayuki."

"Of course!" Tomiko cried, so that her voice was carried down the cliffs by the wind and Michi almost began to cry from fright. "Of course there is. Nagayuki's English is perfect."

"Japanese jurisprudence is not in demand in the fish canneries of Sitka," Fumiya said with absolute certainty.

Tomiko was afraid to contradict her again, for Fumiya had picked up the next letters from Nagayuki and began to read on.

As Tomiko watched Fumiya's face, she discovered many resemblances to Nagayuki's features that she had not noticed before. Fumiya had the same even, delicately modeled profile as Nagayuki, with its high-bridged straight nose and the same eyes tinged with sadness, slitted under heavy lids. Like Nagayuki, her face came to a point at a well-formed chin. But Fumiya's lips had grown narrow in the last year. Since Nagayuki's departure, the lines around her mouth had noticeably deepened, and her skin seemed to have grown duller, crosshatched by little wrinkles.

Fumiya had finished reading the letters, but instead of dwelling on the apricot trees, of which Nagayuki had written that they filled the valleys of southern California as far as the eye could see, she said, while looking across the town, the bay, and the ocean, "It is always only a few who return from America, and none of the people I have spoken to fills me with confidence."

"But Nagayuki has already seen a great deal of America," Tomiko added with a hint of doubt in her voice. "That's a good sign—isn't it?"

"Not until he writes very clearly what he has been doing in the various places where he stays. He was in San Diego in the south, then farther north . . ."

Fumiya picked up the pile of letters once more and read, ". . . in Santa Barbara. His last letter was sent from the George Russell Apricot Farm in Fresno, obviously not too far from San Francisco. . . ."

Tomiko nodded. By now she knew the map of California by heart, so often had she sat, longing and tears in her eyes, looking for the places where Nagayuki was or where he had told her to send her next letter.

"I have heard," Fumiya said next, "that every autumn in California a wave of migrant laborers travels from the south northward, following the ripening of the fruits. Each week they work on a different ranch, sixteen to eighteen hours a day. At night they sleep on bare boards in sheds or on the ground outdoors under the trees."

"How do you know?" Tomiko asked, suddenly frightened.

Then Fumiya told her that she had gone to Okayama and Hiroshima. "That's where most of the emigrants come from," she explained, "and also from Yamaguchi Prefecture, from the Kii peninsula, and from Kyushu. Wherever famine has raged for generations among the poor farming population, or where many people throng the port cities in search of work—those are the places from which people steam to America. And only a few come back."

She had traveled to Hiroshima and Okayama, she told Tomiko, and looked for such returnees. She had spoken with some of them. She had also seen some who acted as brokers in the harbor of Hiroshima, at the docks or in the bars, trying to persuade unemployed men to emigrate to America, where they could earn good money. The passage was said to be inexpensive. All they had to do was to sign their name and pack their belongings, and they could embark on the ship lying at anchor, ready to sail. It would take them to Kobe, where the honorable American consul would personally give them the visa for America. Afterward the road to riches and renown was wide open. Only courage, a few muscles, and a spirit of enterprise were required. In a few years, so the brokers promised, all of them would return to Japan dressed in brocade.

Tomiko listened to Fumiya's descriptions with breathless astonishment. "To Hiroshima and Okayama, down to the docks—you dared to go there, just like that? Wasn't it very dangerous?"

"No one will harm an old woman," Fumiya replied, smiling. "And I wore a very shabby kimono, so that no one could have told me apart from a peasant woman."

"But your hands give you away, and your speech—the way you speak—they've surely never heard that there."

"Those people paid no attention to my hands. Also, I kept quiet. I used my eyes to see the gray reality of this world," Fumiya replied. "I spoke only once, when I visited the father of one of those who had returned from America. The son is now an active broker in the harbor of Hiroshima."

"What did this father tell you?"

"He was very proud that his son had come back from America with a fat bundle of dollars, which he wore strapped around his stomach. He kept raving about the amount of yen the bank had given his son for them. When I asked him how his son had earned all that money, he readily told me that his son had been overseer on a ranch and had enjoyed the full confidence of his white master. Every day he rode his horse through the ranch and made sure the work went briskly. He had as many as three hundred Japanese workers under him, and for every workman who did his job well, the overseer was paid half a dollar a week. Now it was his business to send many more strong Japanese to America for his white master, and for every one he could deliver to the ranch, he was given fifty dollars in cash."

Michi was feeling neglected and showed her displeasure by screaming. At that, Fumiya suggested it might be well to eat first and to drink. She unpacked what she had brought. Michi sucked at her bottle with pleasure.

Fumiya could not eat. Tomiko ate a little. Between bites she said, "There may be people such as you saw in the harbor of Hiroshima, but Nagayuki's path does not cross the paths of such people. After all, Nagayuki traveled first class."

"But in America it was necessary for him to earn his keep very soon. The amount he brought from home cannot have lasted more than three days."

"But that was why he had letters of recommendation from the mayor of Himari and even from the prefectural chairman," Tomiko objected.

"I don't know whether they are a great help in America. What is the use of letters of recommendation written on rice paper with artful brushstrokes which no one in America can read? Himari is a small town, and no one ever heard of our prefecture on the other side of the Pacific. And to whom should Nagayuki have turned in California?"

Tomiko was about to say, "The governor," when she had to admit to herself that this was an idea only Father could consider reasonable. She began to realize that Fumiya's worries about Nagayuki were much closer to reality than the hopes to which she herself still clung. Nagayuki was entirely alone in an alien land. Neither his ancestry nor his education would smooth his path.

108

When Fumiya said, "The talk about how the streets in America are paved with gold—that's all a lie," Tomiko nodded and admitted, "I've given it some thought, too. Nagayuki would have been back a long time ago if he could have plucked money from the trees so easily."

"To earn a lot of money in America, a man needs to be hard. He must be inconsiderate of everyone else, and he must be cruel of heart," Fumiya said. "Nagayuki is none of these. I am deeply worried about him."

In reply, Tomiko timidly objected that matters could not be so very bad for Nagayuki, for he had just sent the considerable sum of money that had enabled Father Hayato to pay for the entire Noh performance in the Omiya shrine. "Actually, the money was for me and Michi to travel to America." Tomiko laid her arm across her face in order to conceal her eyes.

Fumiya nodded. "Precisely that shows that he is not faring well in America. In any case, not so well that he could risk returning to Himari before long. He knows the expectations attached to his return, and he knows that he cannot meet them."

"But I did not write him that we no longer live in the old house."

"That doesn't change anything. The whole town expects him to return dressed in brocade."

"I know," Tomiko sighed and pressed Michi closer. "He has to bring back more money than the tattooed Eda, the son of the dockworker."

"There's another man I don't trust," Fumiya said.

Tomiko's eyes searched for the photograph she had earlier handed to Fumiya together with Nagayuki's letters and which Fumiya had given only a swift glance. Because Tomiko felt a little hurt that Fumiya paid so little attention to the picture, she picked it up again and held it out to Fumiya, saying, "But here he looks so proud and free in his elegant suit, and he is standing in a broad avenue with large trees and noble houses. He cannot be faring so ill."

Without looking at the picture, Fumiya placed her hand on

Tomiko's and spoke in a voice so low as to be almost inaudible. "All of them send the same photograph. In Hiroshima and Okayama I saw dozens of these pictures. The brokers were carrying thick bundles of them, eager to show them to anyone willing to let himself be recruited. 'You too will look so elegant and so noble, once you've spent a year in America,' they repeat time and again. I asked to see some of the photographs, and I saw that most of them were taken in the same place, in the same avenue with the same tall trees. All the men who posed there held a cane in one hand and a hat in the other. A watch chain ran across their chests. I noticed that if the men were short, their coat sleeves hung down below their wrists, while for the taller men they ended above the cuffs and you could see white socks under the edge of the trousers. This made me conclude that the photographer had only one suit, in which he dressed all his customers."

15

Mother died in the night, while all were asleep. Tomiko was exhausted from weeks of special care. These duties, coming on top of the housework and the sewing necessary for bare survival, drained her energies hour after hour. At night she lay as if unconscious, and dreamlessly she suffered through the few hours' sleep.

That same night the Noh mask fell off the wall and lay on the ground, grinning, its features turned upward, but undamaged.

Tomiko, who was the first to wake and to notice that Mother had stopped breathing, quickly looked over at Father, to see if he was awake. But Hayato was asleep, his mouth slightly open, and did not yet know that Mother was dead. Tomiko picked up the mask and replaced it on the wall. As she was adjusting it and looking at it, she noticed a trace of sorrow around its lips. The dead eyes, which could stare so wildly in broad daylight, suddenly looked grieving.

Tomiko was twenty-three years old.

Father Hayato dressed carefully and went into town to negotiate for a loan with the bank, so that he could give his wife an honorable burial.

In the old days he had sent for the bank officials to come to his home, and he had received them in a small side chamber, where he took care of all money matters.

"This is an impure place," he used to say, for everything to do with money he considered impure. He was proud of the fact—and mentioned it conversationally now and again—that his hands had never directly touched money. That was why the bank officials had to bring money in envelopes marked on the outside with the amount of yen each contained. Father never opened an envelope to count the money, he was averse even to the sight of money.

"The sound of metal on metal which reaches the ear of the samurai must only be the clatter of swords crossed in battle," he said whenever he was present while the coins in someone's pocket rattled. The servants in his house, well aware of this stricture, wrapped any coins they carried in cotton cloths and tucked them under their sashes, so that, as they moved, the money made no noise.

The bank gave Father Hayato a loan for the desired amount; the death of his wife was a special event. Because of this circumstance, the bank gave him credit one more time, although it had long ago stopped considering him a good credit risk.

"My son will settle the matter from America," Father Hayato said when he signed the document. He made the officials give him the money in the usual envelopes, and he casually swept them from the counter into the pouch he had brought.

The funeral was held in the hillside cemetery. The mourners came from the town and the surroundings of Himari, from far along the coast and inland, from everywhere where members of the Hayato clan had settled or where former servants of the house of Hayato were living. All were dressed in black kimonos to take part in the last rites of Mother's interment. Tomiko asked

112

their old gardener, who had found a job with the town administration after the fall of the house of Hayato, to hold the tray on which the guests placed their condolence envelopes with the black-and-white bands.

She spent the following day opening the many envelopes, making a list of the names and the amount of each enclosed sum. While Tomiko was compiling the list and making a pile of the money, Father Hayato took little Michi to the beach, so that, as he said, the vastness of the ocean and the sight of the cliffs where the surf broke might restore his inner calm.

Next to the name of each donor and the amount of the donation Tomiko immediately entered the return gift that seemed to her appropriate and equivalent in value. She put down whatever she could think of next to the various names: a lacquer bowl, a porcelain vase, a tea service, a roll of kimono silk, a set of bath towels and soap, five glasses with coasters, and other objects suitable for return gifts. When she had finished the long list, she once more compared the amounts and the value of the gifts which she had to buy and give in return. She took care that two donors who lived near each other or who had very close family ties would not receive the same objects as return gifts, but also none too obviously differing in value.

During the next few weeks, Tomiko spent many hours, which she had to wrest from her housework, in town and bought all the gifts. She wrote down exactly how much she spent. But before she came to the end of her list, the money was gone. Her heart heavy, she waited for Father to leave the house, and when she was alone in the room with Michi, she opened the bottom drawer of her sewing box, where she hoarded the money she had saved up. She had to take out almost everything she had put by in the last year to keep her mother's memory from being damaged by cheap and unworthy return gifts.

After the forty-ninth day, Tomiko went to the post office with return gifts for those of the mourning guests who had come from far away. She began to pay her formal gratitude calls on all those who lived in Himari or close by.

In this way she made her first visit to Rin's dwelling. Rin lived on the second floor of a narrow house in town. Downstairs there was a vegetable store, where Rin worked behind the counter. When she saw Tomiko approaching, Rin quickly wiped her hands on her apron and bowed very low. She begged Tomiko to enter and led her up the steep stairs to the upper story, where she lived with her son in a narrow, long room. The whole room seemed friendly and bright because of the shoji-screened windows on both of the short sides. The screens stood open to let in some cooler air.

Rin offered Tomiko a silk floor pillow after first removing a white slipcover from it. Then she went to the little kitchen and brought hot water. With her powerful hands, she prepared tea. Among the four or five tea bowls Tomiko saw standing on the shelf, there was one of remarkable beauty. Rin gave Tomiko that one. She herself drank from a simple stoneware goblet, but not until Tomiko had raised her bowl to her lips. Tomiko wondered how often her father might have sat here. Many things in this room pointed to his occasional presence—the single silk floor pillow with its slipcover, the single good tea bowl, and the painted round fan, which Rin brought. Probably the same way she always did for Father Hayato, she fanned Tomiko, for the day was warm and, because she was in mourning, Tomiko was wearing her heavy dark kimono.

"I owe your honorable mother everything I have here," Rin said, her head bowed slightly. "Your lady mother was very good to me when"—Rin searched for the right word—"when I had to leave the beautiful old home of the Hayato family."

"I know," Tomiko said simply. Then she unknotted the silk scarf in which she had wrapped the gift for Rin.

"You put me to shame," Rin mumbled, gesturing the gift away.

"It is in remembrance," Tomiko replied.

Rin's eyes filled with tears. "I'd be happy to work for you . . . anytime . . . without pay, of course," she added quickly. "Please let me know when you need me."

When Tomiko had already said good-bye and had already gone down the stairs, Rin's son burst in to the vegetable shop from the street. Breathlessly he asked whether he might go with the other boys down to the harbor, where a magician had set up his booth. Tomiko gave the boy a startled look. His features bore an unmistakable and astonishing resemblance to Hayato, her father. Only his large round eyes were a heritage from Rin. Tomiko knew that the boy was ten years old and was named Gen. The way he pressed himself against Rin to coax her, and the way Rin gave her permission to go to the harbor while affectionately stroking his hair, showed Tomiko that a loving relationship existed between the two.

When, later, at home, Tomiko observed her father drinking a bowl of thin tea before supper, all the while thoughtfully holding the earthenware bowl in both hands, she had a vision of Rin's room and her father sitting there, the tea bowl in his hands, his calm eyes watching the son he had begotten who tied him to Rin.

Somehow Tomiko felt relieved finally to have seen the ten-year-old Gen. Until now she had had only a vague idea of how her father's son might look. Now that she had met him, she even felt some joy for her father that he possessed such a handsome, likable son.

The weeks that followed required Tomiko to pay numerous courtesy calls to people to whom for the most part nothing bound her but a memory of her mother or to relatives who, chattering officiously under the guise of concern, hinted at tormenting questions. All this time Tomiko thought only rarely of Nagayuki. It was as if she wanted to avoid letting her worries about him grow too large.

That was why she was almost frightened when one day a large package arrived from America. She rubbed her hand across the tarred packing paper, which felt quite different from any paper she had ever touched. She rubbed her hand over the multiple knots in the cord and had a very palpable vision of Nagayuki

115

somewhere in a strange room kneeling on the floor and with his own hands knotting the rope.

While Michi stood by, her eyes big and round, admiring the huge package, Tomiko began to fiddle with the knots and cord ends, to figure out how to undo them. She did not intend opening the box before her father returned, but she began to loosen some of the knots and removed the first strings. Michi came running with the scissors she had taken from Tomiko's sewing box, but Tomiko told her gently, "No, your father knotted these ropes himself. We must not cut them."

When Father Hayato finally returned, Michi ran to meet him and pulled him excitedly into the room. Then Tomiko loosened even the last knots and pulled the cord, which she had already partially rolled up, out from under the package. She removed the outer, waterproof wrapping and then the inner, crepelike paper, gradually exposing the thick-walled carton. It contained three dresses for Michi, each also carefully wrapped in paper. Their glowing array of color took Tomiko's breath away. Then a large doll appeared, also dressed splendidly, with movable arms and legs, golden-yellow hair, and blue eyes that clapped shut as soon as Tomiko laid the doll in Michi's arms. At the same time the doll said, "Mama," which transported Michi into raptures of joy. For the rest of the day she busied herself sitting the doll upright and laying it down again to hear it say, "Mama."

The American carton also held candy and cookies, too. Whenever Tomiko, sampling, opened one of the many gaily covered square or round tin boxes, the whole room became scented with unknown spices. Tomiko noticed at once that some small boxes were provided with glued labels on which Naga-yuki's graceful, accurate script had written, "For Mother's Health." One box held pine nuts, another raisins, a third various little bags with herb teas, giving off strong and bitter scents.

Tomiko picked the boxes up in both hands, lowered her head, and closed her eyes. Then she placed the boxes before the small ancestors' shrine in the corner of the room, where since

Mother's death fresh water and rice were placed for her daily. Father Hayato also bowed deeply before the shrine.

Later, when Tomiko had put away everything that had been spread on the tatami mats, had carefully smoothed and folded every piece of wrapping and packing paper, Michi crawled into the empty carton with her doll and insisted on sleeping there the whole night. On the outside of the carton fat letters in Latin script proclaimed:

George Russell's Apricot Farm
Napa Valley, California

Then Tomiko thought again about the flowering apricot trees that transformed an entire valley into a sea of color. But the depressing picture Fumiya had sketched for her of the workers on these enormous orchards came between her and her vision like a dark cloud. Tomiko clung to the thought that Nagayuki could not be so very badly off, since he had just sent so many and so clearly expensive presents.

The following week brought a money order from Nagayuki, and a letter in which he explained that the sum was intended to contribute to Mother's speedy recovery. Surely the expenses for nurses, for the doctor's visits, and for medication must be very heavy, so that his modest contribution could be of only small help. Here in America, he wrote, the doctors were very good but very expensive. Anyone who was not in need of medical help was fortunate. These hints were sufficient to tell Tomiko with certainty that Nagayuki must have been very ill. He could have died, all alone in a strange land. A scalding wave of fear rose in Tomiko, dominating her thoughts entirely for several minutes. She had only one goal: to travel to America and Nagayuki as soon as possible.

The money Nagayuki had sent for Mother's recovery was enough to cover the funeral costs. When the sum was remitted from the central office, the bank immediately kept the amount it had loaned to Father Hayato. Father used the remainder to rent a house in a better residential section of town. He announced to Tomiko, "Tomorrow we are moving."

The new house was more spacious. There were two rooms on the ground floor, and between the kitchen and the bathroom there was an anteroom where one could wash. A narrow superstructure bestrode the gable like the roof of a pagoda. A steep ladder led up to it. The upper room was airy and large; it extended over the whole depth of the building. A fairly large garden was also attached to the house.

Soon after they moved, Father Hayato told Tomiko that he would bring Rin into the house so that they would have a servant again. Rin, he said, had a son. His name was Gen, Father mentioned in passing. Gen was sure to be a good playmate for Michi.

16

Tomiko used the dresses Nagayuki had sent Michi from America as patterns for her own sewing. She was especially impressed by the laces and ruffles attached to the collars and cuffs or even to the skirts and below, at the hems. Of course she could not buy such laces and ruffles in Himari, especially not by the yard. But this style of American children's clothing gave her the idea of cutting simple printed kimono fabrics into narrow strips, hemming them on both sides, and sewing the resulting ribbons onto the monotone fabrics which she mainly used for her children's dresses. She varied the color combinations, sometimes merely placing a colored ribbon at the hem of the skirt and another at the throat. Another time she accented the waist with a colored band and sewed a large colorful bow on the bodice of the dress.

Tomiko's dresses sold so quickly that she could not sew

enough of them. She tried to teach Rin the simpler stitches, but try as she might, Rin was awkward at handling a needle.

Rin could not imagine how the oddly cut pieces of material could emerge as a dress with sleeves, for she was familiar only with kimonos made up of straight, long strips of cloth, in which no curve or arc was ever cut. She always laughed at the "pipes," as she called the narrow sleeves tapering toward the wrist, and she confessed that she could never feel comfortable in such clinging garments. But Rin ironed the dresses Tomiko sewed with great skill, for her arms were strong, and she handled the heavy stone-filled iron with ease.

Rin spent much time in the garden, where she put in vegetable beds. Every day she brought fresh spinach or radishes or eggplants to the table. She was also zealous in cleaning the house. She wiped off all the tatami mats with a damp cloth every day, polished the wooden doorposts until they shone, dusted the paper-covered shoji screens, and saw to it that no dust accumulated and no fly left traces on the Hayato ancestral shrine. Every morning Rin rose before the others and, in the small, narrow kitchen, began to cook for the whole day and to prepare hot miso soup for breakfast.

Each day Father Hayato audibly reveled in the luxury of the larger bathroom. Where they had lived before, at the edge of town, the bath had been only a recess where they kept the round iron tub which Mother and later Tomiko had to heat up every evening with logs brought from outside. On top of the water floated a thick, round slab of wood. You had to step carefully on it on entering the tub and push it to the bottom with your own weight. In the new house there was an anteroom to the bath, where every morning Father Hayato poured five buckets full of cold water over himself. And he scrubbed mightily. That was the signal for Tomiko and the children to get up. Michi slept with Father Hayato in the smaller rear room. Rin and Gen slept upstairs, while Tomiko unrolled her mat in the larger front room because most of the time she had to sew late into the night. That was the room, too, where the mask hung on the wall.

Rin straightened up the front room, removed the small sacrificial table with the rice bowl still filled from the previous day and the gray earthenware water container, and carried it into the kitchen. There she poured away the water from the day before, dumped the cold, stale rice into another bowl, wiped the sacrificial table with a damp cloth used only for this purpose, and got everything in readiness for Father Hayato.

When he had finished his morning toilet, he went straight to the kitchen, poured fresh water into the round earthenware consecrated vessel, and with the wooden rice ladle Rin handed him, he lifted the first portion of rice from the hot, steaming kettle. Then Father carried the newly provisioned sacrificial table to the shrine and with a slow, careful motion he pushed it inside through the two little folding doors that stood open. The white steam rising from the hot rice filled the shrine and gave Father the certainty that Mother was close to him in thought. Tomiko and Michi, Rin and Gen also bowed before sitting down to breakfast before the hallowed memorial.

Almost every day Rin's father, a fisherman, sent a reed basket filled with seafood. Most of the time one of Rin's numerous little sisters or brothers brought it, but sometimes Rin's father himself came by and handed the basket to Tomiko with a deep bow. The fisherman's face, marked with deeply etched wrinkles and tanned by sun and salt water, beamed with pride because he was allowed to bring her and her father the fruits of his industry. If, on one of these occasions, he caught sight of Father Hayato, he could hardly speak for awe. He only rubbed his hands in embarrassment and muttered words of gratitude because his daughter Rin had been granted such amiable readmission to the house of Hayato.

Rin's father looked at Gen with shy admiration and often brought him a large shell or a particularly oddly shaped snail casing. Gen, who had turned eleven by now, collected all kinds of shells. He was delighted with every one Rin's father brought him, and he traded them with the other children. Gen also brought home crabs and shrimp, especially those the fishermen could not sell because they were too old and no longer smelled fresh. To remove these creatures' soft parts, Gen had thought up a very individual method. Somewhere at the edge of town he knew of a large anthill. Gen laid the crabs and shrimp on it. After only a few hours, the ants had consumed all the spoiled meat, and Gen could take the empty shells back home. He kept them carefully on a shelf in the upstairs room.

There, too, the gramophone had found a resting place. Tomiko was glad not to have to look at it anymore. Now and then Gen played the single record Mr. Sono had brought from Osaka, but even for him it had long since lost the charm of novelty. When school let out early or on Sundays, Gen walked down to the harbor or the beach, where he spent many hours among the rocks and the flotsam and jetsam that had been washed up. Sometimes he returned with coconuts that had drifted in on the tide from the South Pacific, or with large pieces of cork and bottles that had surely come from passing ships far out in the ocean.

Tomiko dreamed that she could float across the ocean like a cork, all the way to the coast of California, and that Nagayuki would be standing there to take her in his arms.

Since Rin had taken all the housework off her hands and Michi was past the age when she needed diapers, Tomiko could direct all her energy to sewing. In itself, sewing was considered one of the lowliest and worst-paid occupations, but since Tomiko knew how to make children's clothing in the Western style, such as had never before been seen in Himari, she earned quite a bit and was able to lay aside an increasingly large portion of her income. But when she counted up what she had saved in eight months, and figured out whether it would already be enough for her to join Nagayuki, she arrived at the depressing conclusion that her entire savings would barely be able to buy her a second-class ship's passage to Osaka or a third-class ticket to Yokohama. To travel to San Francisco, across the wide Pacific, she would have to save for years and years.

Sometimes, when she added up the expenses for rice, salt and other spices, for tea and rice wine, which Father Hayato enjoyed drinking again, she arrived at the distinct impression that more money had been spent than she had put into the household account. Once she asked Rin if she could explain the difference. At that, Rin made a face as if she had been caught in a bad deed, and stuttering, she confessed to Tomiko, "Sometimes I add a little bit of my own money. It's not really my own money, after all," she added hastily, lowering her head even more. "Everything I have I owe to your honorable Mother Hayato. When Gen was growing in me, she gave me so much money, and she was a good friend to me."

Then she told Tomiko how at the time her mother had opened a proper savings account for her where the money got to be more every year all by itself, without her doing anything for it. This way money had of growing was miraculous to Rin. Never before had she heard that there was such a thing. Rin fiddled with her wide obi, which she wore wound twice over her kimono around her waist. There, in a narrow pocket worked into the sash, she kept the passbook Mother Hayato had given her. She shyly showed it to Tomiko.

Tomiko saw that of the large amount paid in, under which her mother's signature stood next to the bank stamp, Rin had always withdrawn only the interest. It was enough for Rin's and Gen's keep. Now it served the purpose of increasing the household allowance.

Rin also took out the small oval name stamp which, she proudly explained, she always had to take with her to the bank if she wanted to withdraw money from the passbook. "I've always been very careful to make sure that the passbook and the stamp can't be stolen at the same time." She leaned close to Tomiko and whispered, "Nobody but the two of us knows that I have a savings account."

Did Tomiko have a savings account as well, she asked next. For a moment Rin seemed like Tomiko's older sister, advising her to open a savings account. Tomiko thought of the yen she kept hidden in the drawer of her sewing table, where they brought no interest whatever. Perhaps she should bring herself to open a savings account at the bank without her father's knowledge? The more she thought about it, the more tempting the prospect seemed of a savings account of her own, which no one but she herself could dispose of.

Suddenly a new idea went through her head. It was a reckless idea, and it was immediately joined by a guilty conscience. Perhaps, she thought, she could ask Nagayuki secretly to remit his dollars to her own account instead of sending the money to her father. In this way it would be out of Hayato's reach, and she alone, with her passbook and her personal stamp, would be able to withdraw the money. From that moment on, she would be free. She could buy passage for herself and Michi and get on any ship headed for San Francisco.

While Tomiko sat over her sewing until the delicate threads began to swim before her eyes; while she watched Michi, who had still not tired of playing with her jointed doll and took great joy in hearing the doll say "Mama"; while she lay awake at night and tried in vain to recall the physical nearness and the touch of Nagayuki—the thought of the savings bankbook intruded again and again. The idea would not let go of her that all her waiting and longing would come to an end the moment she could dispose of such a passbook filled with many dollars. She could see herself holding the steamship ticket. It seemed as if the ground under her feet were rocking and she was traveling on the ship that would take her to Nagayuki. Three years had already passed since Nagayuki had left for America.

Tomiko's recurring worries consumed her energies. Perhaps Nagayuki would be quite unable to send enough dollars for her and Michi's passage again so soon. As she walked through the streets of Himari to deliver new dresses, Tomiko reflected that perhaps Nagayuki could send her one of those new machines that could be used for sewing. She had heard that such machines were already quite common in America. Tomiko imagined how many more dresses she could sew with one. That meant more income for her. The money she earned she would put into her savings account. Secretly. Then there would be interest.

Tomiko figured out that she would not have to tell Nagayuki precisely what she needed the machine for. He must remember, from when they lived in Tokyo, that she enjoyed sewing. He need never find out that now she was doing it to feed the family; if he did, he would worry about her unnecessarily. With her sewing money, and with the dollars he would send to supplement it, she would be able to join him as soon as next spring.

But then, more and more frequently, doubts colored Tomiko's reflections. She wondered if it was right to do something in secret; even starting her own bank account seemed to her like the beginning of betrayal. From that day on, she would no longer be able to feel one with her father and the ancestors' shrine. She wondered what her mother would say if she could see her now. When she thought of her mother, and of the fact that each night she slept in the same room with the ancestors' shrine, a painful clarity came over her. She knew that she would not be able to act in secret. The passbook would poison the air she breathed. It would stand like a wall between her and her father and make it impossible for her to join him in bowing to the ancestors' shrine. The wickedness would speak to her at night with a thousand voices.

After a few days, however, her decision wavered again. If it was true, as Fumiya said, that Nagayuki's life in America was harsh, her place was at his side. Tomiko softly questioned the darkness at night when she lay awake, and she turned her head toward the ancestors' shrine, its outlines dimly delineated against the pale background of the wall. She asked the ancestors if they might help her. Her father and her ancestors must see, she thought, that a life apart from Nagayuki could not possibly be her destiny.

Then another letter arrived from Nagayuki in which, Tomiko thought, his inner confusion was evident once more. Nagayuki wrote again that Tomiko was to come to America, but there was no ignoring his self-torture, his question whether he was even justified, now that her mother had died, in claiming Tomiko for himself alone.

Tomiko felt how unendurable the idea was to him that her father must live in loneliness in the big house since her mother's death, surrounded only by servants. She felt how much Nagayuki was still aware of himself as a yōshi, whose whole life consisted of proving to his adoptive father that as a son he was willing and able to fulfill the expectations placed in him. Had he not been the adopted son, he would not have had to bow so totally to Father Hayato's will.

Tomiko sat with lowered eyes. She had flipped her long kimono sleeves over her hands to cover her trembling. Her father was reading Nagayuki's letter out loud in his calm, even voice. Tomiko felt a great bitterness rising in her. She was deeply hurt by Nagayuki's evident inability to love her for her own sake. Even now he only thought of her as the daughter of the house of Hayato. But she wanted to be his wife first and foremost. She wanted to belong to him, and she wished Nagayuki would free himself from the role of yōshi. Somewhere deep inside her she felt something like contempt for the soft words and refined phrases in which Nagayuki laid bare his helplessness before their father. This bitter feeling of disappointment engulfed her and threatened to shake her carefully maintained self-control.

Without altering his tone or revealing any sign of bewilderment, Father Hayato read a passage in the letter the meaning of which Tomiko grasped at once. Nagayuki spoke of having a prospect for more steady work, which would put an end to the time of constant wandering. Thus Nagayuki admitted for the first time, though involuntarily, that in the past three years he had been a migrant worker and that surely he must often have had a very bad time.

Abruptly Tomiko realized the misery of the migrant workers, which she had never really been willing to believe, not even after

126

Fumiya had told her of it. She saw the ragged figures, and she saw mounted overseers, high on their horses, spurring the men on with their whips. Above the whole scene hung the stench of rotten fish. Swarms of gulls swooped down to the sea to snatch the offal from the fish-canning factory. The rocks and glaciers along the coast of Alaska disappeared behind a cloud of swirling pink-and-white flower petals. A storm swept through the valley of the flowering apricot trees, tearing the blossoms from the branches. Underneath the stripped trees lay Nagayuki's body, delicate and battered. Her fear for Nagayuki's life swallowed all the bitterness she had felt only a moment ago. Tomiko was sorry that she had allowed her thoughts to reproach Nagayuki.

Father was still reading aloud, page after page. His voice filled the room. He sat upright, holding the closely written letter with both hands. The paper Nagayuki used was dull and hard. Its rustle, too, was quite different from that of Japanese rice paper. Father carefully smoothed out the folds, and as he finished each page, he laid it carefully aside. He lowered and raised his voice as if Nagayuki's letter were a Noh passage he was solemnly reciting.

Nagayuki informed them that he hoped soon to be able to send more money to Himari. In an intricately convoluted style, he combined this announcement with the request to be reunited with Tomiko soon. In the same breath he apologized for his very request.

When he had finished, Father folded up each separate sheet. Then he laid them in a pile and together pushed them back in the envelope. For a long time he gazed at the envelope, smiling happily. Then he rose and, as always, carried Nagayuki's letter to the ancestors' shrine. There he placed it in such a way that the writing on the envelope pointed toward the shrine and returned to his seat. He looked at Tomiko lovingly.

"Nagayuki is a good son after all," he said warmly. "I have no doubts. Soon he will return, dressed in brocade."

 **17**

The plain, tall box of light-colored poplar wood with the fitted lid which Father Hayato brought back from town one day signaled to Tomiko the arrival of more money from Nagayuki.

His expression cheerful, Father carefully placed the box on the tatami mats in the large room and said, "Tomiko, look."

Michi came running at once and asked Father Hayato, "Did you bring me something?"

Lovingly he bent down to her and drew her to him. "This time not for you, but something wonderful for all of us."

"Open it," Michi begged.

Sitting, Father Hayato undid the loop by which he had carried the package and slipped off the string. Then he opened the lid and waited until Tomiko had laid her sewing aside to watch.

He removed the white cloth that had been placed protectively over the contents of the box. Then, very deliberately, he pulled out a large porcelain vase. Tomiko involuntarily cried out, for she recognized it at once as the Nabeshima vase from the old Hayato mansion. It had been a family heirloom, and its loss had been particularly disheartening to her father.

The vase had an unusual, perhaps unique form, with a cup-shaped, outward-turned base and a swelling bulge toward the upper end, topped by a small, narrow neck. Against the milky-white background, some bamboo shoots, the trunk of a pine and, very pale, a flowering plum branch stood out in blue paint. The green of the tuft of pine needles combined with the mandarin red of the plum blossom and the blue strokes into a strangely glowing elegance.

Father's face reflected the joy he felt. "I saw our Nabeshima vase several months ago in the curiosity shop," he said mysteriously. "And now I have brought it home."

He fell into silent contemplation, pressing Michi close until she struggled free and ran back to her doll.

"Next time," Father Hayato said without turning his head, "I'll bring back the gray falcon. The curiosity dealer knows perfectly well that no one in Himari has enough taste to do proper honor to a scroll painted by Sesshu."

Father carefully picked up the Nabeshima vase with both hands, and, without supporting himself against the ground, sprang upright. "That is why he reserved the gray falcon for me," he added happily over his shoulder to Tomiko while, still clutching the vase in both hands, he stood before the closed sliding door to the back room.

Rin rushed in, a muttered apology on her lips, and quickly opened the door, kneeling on the tatami mats. She begged Father Hayato's forgiveness for her lack of diligence.

For a long time, contemplative silence reigned in Hayato's room. Then there was the soft rustle of paper, and a few moments later Father's daily Noh chanting rang out, today a trace more cheerful and energetic than usual.

The following day tradesmen arrived, carrying many bolts of kimono fabric into the house. Wearing a stern, critical expression, Father Hayato took his place on his silk floor pillow. He crossed his arms to express the contempt he felt for all tradespeople, through whose hands crude money flowed every day. He ordered them to bring in more and more bolts and to unroll them before him.

The dealers moved with short, tripping steps, with zealous haste. The master barked orders to his assistants whenever he wanted them to hand him another bolt, and the assistants crouched even further, moving like cringing shadows. The master let the fabric glide through his fingers and, head lowered, waited for a sign from Father Hayato whether to place the bolt on the good side or the bad.

In terse but not unfriendly tones, Father gave his instructions. As always, he made his decision after a single glance, thus proving an assured taste. As Tomiko watched in mounting horror, the more expensive fabrics in the collection began to pile up on the approved side, while Father Hayato, with infallible instinct, eliminated the lower-priced though equally attractive fabrics. He firmly forbade any quotation of price from the dealer.

Finally, Father ordered three exquisite silk kimonos in subdued colors for Tomiko, one kimono of mixed wool and silk in glowing scarlet for Michi, and a dark-blue silk kimono with an interwoven pattern of white checks for Gen. Even Rin was given a kimono of printed silk and three white aprons. Finally Father Hayato felt that he himself might perhaps acquire three new kimonos.

In vain Tomiko tried to dissuade him from ordering—at least the three kimonos for her. "Nagayuki wrote me, you know, that I don't need kimonos in America. The women there wear Western clothes," she whispered to her father, so that the tradesmen would not hear her.

"But Nagayuki will be returning soon," her father replied.

130

"And you must be beautifully dressed for the welcoming ceremony."

It was always this way for her father. The matter-of-factness with which, thinking only of what would be best for Tomiko, he directed her irresistibly toward his own views brooked no escape. She was left with the dull sensation of having been conquered. But still she did not give in. Deep resentment against her father flooded her whole being.

At the same time she knew that Hayato was invulnerable to any resentment, for he felt entirely pure and good at heart. Given his way of thinking, recognition tinged with self-reproach must seem absurd.

Tomiko knew that she would never succeed in making it clear to him that she wished to live her life differently from the way he determined it for her. She was now twenty-five years old and was beginning to suspect that she would never be able to make up the lost years. Until now she had avoided such thoughts, but she was beginning to see more clearly.

Tomiko opened an account at the bank with everything she had saved so far. She stopped considering only part of the money she earned by sewing as her own and spending the rest on the household. In cool, factual tones she informed her father that she would need housekeeping money. Hayato was delighted. He said, "That's good. You shall not have to sew anymore."

But Tomiko redoubled her efforts to sew as many dresses as possible and to sell them at a good profit in the town. However, the high point of her earning capacity had already passed. By now several other women in the town had begun to copy Tomiko's design; they were sewing similar dresses and selling them all over town. Tomiko's earnings sank from week to week and soon fell to a point where it no longer made sense to go on working at all.

Tomiko wondered whether to write Nagayuki that he should

no longer send his next payment to her father but pay it directly to the name of her own bank account. But then she realized the risk that one of the bank employees might gossip about the arrival of such a large sum in her account. Tomiko had to expect that this would not remain a secret from her father, for he continued to meet frequently with the Friends of Noh, and among them there were sure to be some whose ears were open to the town's rumors. As head of the family, her father could withdraw the money from Tomiko's account anytime he wanted to. That was why Tomiko must do all she could to keep her account inconspicuous, so that it would not be talked about, and its existence brought to her father's notice.

It would be safer, she thought, if Nagayuki were to send the money to Fumiya—even granting the danger that the news of the remittance of a considerable sum of money from America to Fumiya's account would spread like the wind through the city. That would be a blow against Father Hayato, for the people in Himari would say that Hayato's yōshi's heart still belonged to the Ogasawaras, while the noble Father Hayato was living in poverty. All the inhabitants of Himari would mock her father behind his back, and Nagayuki would be seen in a bad light, too.

That was why the most important question for Tomiko was whether it was proper in the first place to ask Nagayuki to send money to Fumiya. He would probably not be prepared to compromise his duty as a yōshi with such a tactless act when until now he had not even dared to send so much as a letter to his real mother. That was how exacting Nagayuki was about his obligations as a yōshi. In years gone by, Tomiko had hardly given a thought to Nagayuki's attitude. Now and then it had seemed a nuisance or merely annoying that Nagayuki was overconscientious in these matters. Tomiko had seen it as the consequence of his everlasting concern with samurai lore, a dedication he demanded of himself. But she had learned that it was not too difficult for her to distract him whenever she wanted to. She had never tried to release Nagayuki from his bonds to their father. She herself had not yet reached the point of wanting to free herself from her father. Now, by opening her own secret bank account, she had taken the first step.

Tomiko was frightened when she realized how quickly she was now ready to take the second giant step and persuade Nagayuki to remit the next passage money to Fumiya's account. Fumiya would surely be quite willing to participate in this plan—but would Nagayuki agree to her suggestion? Tomiko did not know.

18

When the pale light of the moon and the stars fell on the paper-covered shojis, so that the pattern of the narrow wooden slats that met at right angles contrasted with the luminescent pale-gray planes of the covering, or when dawn lent the shojis a milky-white glow which slowly mingled with the red of the eastern sky, then Tomiko's eyes often jumped back and forth between the mask on the wall and the ancestors' shrine in the corner. As she looked at the mask, she felt ever more crushed and threatened. Only the presence of the shrine promised a little security.

Tomiko often thought about her mother and about how they had never really talked. Even when she was carrying Michi and was slowly realizing that the life growing in her body was emotionally uniting her more closely than ever before with her mother, she could not find the words to break through the silence dammed up between them. Instead, her thoughts seemed paralyzed by fear as the day of Nagayuki's departure drew closer. It could be, too, that deep inside she had developed a resentment against her mother because she had not unconditionally taken Tomiko's side. She had been no help to Tomiko in her efforts to prevent Nagayuki's leaving.

Tomiko never knew whether her mother really believed what she said. Too often the words she spoke were only those of Father Hayato, which she only repeated. But on her lips Father's words lacked the conviction they carried when he himself uttered them. Looking back, Tomiko understood that she had never doubted her father's pronouncements until she heard them echoed by her mother.

When Father Hayato spoke, rebellious feelings simply could not arise. He knew how to clothe his inflexibility in benevolence; he never gave orders brusquely. But his very presence prevented anyone in his household from thinking differently and wanting anything different.

Nevertheless, Tomiko sensed a silent force streaming at her from the ancestors' shrine, where her mother's soul lived. And this force strengthened her determination to write Nagayuki soon to send the next remittance to Fumiya. While her lips soundlessly formed the words she would use to try to explain to Nagayuki why he must no longer send money to Father, the mask intruded, grinning, as if to say, "You'll never manage to drive a wedge between Nagayuki and Father Hayato."

Over and over Tomiko's thoughts clung to the image of the horror that would spread over Nagayuki's features when he read her crucial letter. Then perhaps the pages on which she had written her momentous words would glide from his fingers, and his hands, which had so tenderly caressed her body, would ball into fists. His lips, which had so often touched her skin with warmth and gentleness, would curse either Tomiko or Father.

When she looked again at the ancestors' shrine, both folding doors seemed tightly shut, no hope flowing from them any longer. Tomiko did not dare to turn her head toward the mask, for she knew that the spiteful grin still nested in the empty eye sockets.

Then she buried her face in the pillow and pulled the coverlet all the way over herself. At the same time she felt stirring deep inside her the wish that Nagayuki's curse should fall, not on her father, but on herself. That, she thought, would be the best thing for Nagayuki; for since he had been taken into the Hayato family as its yōshi, he had always struggled to win Father's recognition. These fifteen years could not be undone. If, as Fumiya feared, Nagayuki had had to suffer much misery in the four years he had now been in America, then he had done so fully aware that he was undergoing the yōshi's testing period.

Tomiko knew that Nagayuki would have preferred taking the other path offered him after his brilliant final examinations at Todai. The agents from Mitsui, from Sumitomo, from Toyo Textiles, and from the Yokohama Bank had sought him out. Each had competed with the others to win the top graduate of Todai for his firm. Tomiko smiled painfully when she recalled Nagayuki's exuberance and enthusiasm as he told her about each of these visits.

"Now we'll go to Himari—we'll go at once," he had said. "And we'll let Father decide which I should accept. They're the very best."

After he had declared himself ready to submit his life as a yōshi to Father Hayato's decision by leaving for America, Tomiko could not now expect him to reverse his nature and act in a way that was plainly directed against Father. So she would not be able to write him to send money to Fumiya.

Hardly had this realization taken root in her than anger forced its way through. She remembered that Nagayuki had also failed to support her effectively enough in her attempt to change her father's mind. Perhaps, after all, he thought of me only as a troublesome, discontented wife, Tomiko thought; a woman who is moody because she is pregnant. And yet, if there had been a true understanding between us, we could have used my pregnancy to persuade him.

Tomiko was quite certain that Father would not have driven Nagayuki from the house once he knew that she was carrying his yōshi's child. Without the pregnancy, he might well have marched down to the Bureau of Families and—well within his rights as head of the family—asked to have Nagayuki's name stricken from the list of Hayatos. He need give no reason beyond "unworthy behavior on the part of the yōshi." A line of the brush and a rubber stamp—nothing more would be necessary to erase Nagayuki.

But Father would not have done so at the time, not even if Nagayuki had firmly and decidedly resisted Hayato's wish to send him to America. It would only have been a postponement of a year, for by then, at the latest, Nagayuki was supposed to go to America anyway—on behalf of Mitsui, Sumitomo, Toyo Textiles, or the Yokohama Bank, whichever he would have decided to join.

Tomiko wept at the thought that Nagayuki had now been in America for more than four years and that three years ago she and Michi could have gone to him. The company in whose favor Nagayuki would have decided would have taken care of all travel expenses, for after his graduation from Todai, Nagayuki was such a desirable man that he would have been certain of the highest promotions. Over her tears Tomiko forgot that she should really be angry at Nagayuki.

At breakfast Gen looked at Tomiko repeatedly. He did nothing to conceal the worry in his eyes. Tomiko felt that Gen was the only one at the table to notice her tearstained eyes and that he harbored a secret affection for her.

Gen had grown into a very strong boy. In school he distinguished himself especially at judo and was considered the most capable boy in his class. His resemblance to Father Hayato had become rather more pronounced in the time since Tomiko had first met him. His large, round eyes, which he had inherited from Rin, made him look more childlike than he was in his mind and feelings.

He enjoyed playing with Michi, and did so often. Most of the time he picked her up and carried her around the room or—a game Michi always welcomed jubilantly—threw her with a quick judo hold on the tatami mats. But he made very certain that she never hurt herself. What Michi enjoyed most of all, however, was when Gen rocked her in his arms as if she were a doll. At the right moment she closed her eyes and called out, "Mama," just like her doll from America.

Rin brought the news from town that an ocean voyage was being arranged to take many women to their husbands in America. She mentioned the report casually, while serving dinner. Tomiko asked Rin warily whether she knew any details.

"Yes," Rin answered. "My father says that the tattooed Eda, the one who lives in the house with the six pillars, has something to do with it."

Father Hayato looked up. For a moment, dark shadows overcast his usually serene face. "That is not proper mealtime conversation," he said with calm but ominous finality.

Rin quickly murmured, "Excuse me," and looked at him in fear.

Tomiko, too, cast a quick glance at her father. She saw that, though he was smiling, he was fruitlessly struggling against his annoyance. His eyes, which usually radiated benevolent good-will, had narrowed and lost their astounding softness.

Tomiko knew that her father did not wish to hear Eda's name. It called up painful memories. The longer Nagayuki's return was delayed, the more brilliant did Eda's reputation appear to the people of the town. He had been the first to return to Himari dressed in brocade. He had established a lasting memorial to his name when he donated a judo hall to the town; it had long since come to be known as Eda Hall. In the meantime, it was said, this man Eda had been back to America several times; sometimes for only a brief period, sometimes for several months. Always he returned with many dollars, and always he saw to it that a grand party celebrated his homecoming.

Tomiko heard about it every time, and she suffered from the feeling that all over town Nagayuki was being compared to this Eda person. She was not certain whether Father took any cognizance of the repeated celebrations in Eda's honor. Sometimes it seemed to her that Father knew precisely whenever Eda came back from America and where the banquet was being held. At those times he would not leave the house for days; he spent the hours endlessly chanting Noh passages or quietly secluding himself in the back room.

It had been Eda, too, who had acquired the loveliest orange grove on the Hayato property after misfortune had first befallen Father. He had had most of the orange trees cut down and had used the old grove to build an expensive house in the Western style, its front entrance framed by six pillars. Lately the rumor had begun to circulate that Eda was interested in the venerable old Hayato mansion itself. The house was still standing empty, its closed storm shutters forbidding, and weeds proliferating all around.

That was why the mention of Eda's name transported Father into an agitation he could suppress only with difficulty. He took his tea bowl in both hands and guided it to his lips with particular care. He sipped his tea more slowly than usual while he kept his eyes closed. Then he placed the bowl back on the table with the inimitable dignified gesture so characteristic of him.

After dinner Tomiko joined Rin in the kitchen to ask more about this planned journey of the women to America.

Rin, who had pinned her kimono sleeves high to wash the dishes, was clearly delighted to be allowed to spread her news after all. "Well, there's this man who's tattooed all over, on his arms and his chest. Eda, the son of the dockworker Eda, whose father hasn't had to work at the docks for a long time, though, because the son has such a lot of money."

139

"I know all that," Tomiko said. "But when does the ship leave?"

"The ship?" Rin repeated. "Oh, yes—the ship. I don't know that. But down at the harbor they say Eda brings back a lot of money from America. Each time, a lot of money. And now a lot of photographs. Photographs of men. A lot of women are willing to marry those men."

"Where?" Tomiko asked.

"Everywhere," Rin said. "In Himari and other places. The women don't have to pay to travel to America. The men have paid for everything. In dollars."

"Who told you all this?" Tomiko pressed on.

"My brother," Rin stuttered. "Eda himself told my sister. Everybody at the docks knows. A lot of money." Rin nodded, impressed by her own words. "Big money."

19

When Tomiko went to the house with the six pillars, the orange trees were still in bloom and spread their intoxicating scent. Children's shouts came from the house. They fell silent as Tomiko stepped under the portico supported by the six stone pillars that looked like the pillars of many American houses Tomiko had seen in photographs. Several children were looking through the windows and the entrance door. Inside, someone was sweeping the floor with a straw broom.

The old dockworker came to the door with shuffling steps and asked Tomiko what she wanted. When Tomiko replied that she wished to speak to his son, the old man nodded in an almost surly way. He muttered, "Son is not here." He shouted loudly for someone to run down to the docks to fetch his son, for he had a visitor. Tomiko could barely make out the words, although the old man spoke with a Himari accent.

The old woman, Eda's mother, appeared in the dark doorway and bowed to Tomiko.

"Come inside," said the old dockworker in a cracked voice, leading the way. Eda's mother stepped aside without a word and walked behind Tomiko. Children jostled each other in the hall to get the closest possible view of Tomiko.

The room to which they led Tomiko was crammed with furniture. At the center stood a high-legged rectangular table with eight chairs, and all the walls were covered with pictures of America—printed posters, oil paintings of mountains and blue waters, and many, many group photographs.

"My son," the old dockworker said when he saw that the photographs drew Tomiko's attention. "My son." The old man pointed to a figure that could be seen in each of the pictures, high astride a horse or sitting on a stool at the center of a group of other Japanese men, standing by with open shirts and sleeves rolled up. Most of them wore broad-brimmed hats, some were holding spades or supporting one foot on a basket piled high with fruit. Eda, the son, sat with his legs spread wide. In some pictures he held a whip. The tattoos on his arms and chest were usually very clear. "My son," the old man repeated for each picture, pointing his blunt finger at the central figure. "My son."

In the meantime, the old woman brought tea and set down two cups on the table. "Tea?" she mumbled indistinctly and tried to smile. The play of her features miscarried, for she was not sure how to behave toward Tomiko. Surely never before had a visitor of such striking beauty and dignity entered her home. Tomiko, in thanking her, used plain, simple words, so as not to confuse the old woman by the use of etiquette formulas she could not know.

"Tea?" she asked and filled Tomiko's cup to the rim. It was a porcelain cup, painted with roses, with a handle and a saucer. The rim was edged with a narrow gold band. "From America," the old woman said proudly and pointed to the cup, the teapot, the table, the chairs.

"From America," the old dockworker said as well, pointing to the many cut-glass prisms that made up the chandelier above the table. "From America," he repeated, nodding with satisfaction. "My son."

Tomiko heard rapid steps approaching. The door flew open, and suddenly Eda stood in the room. His eyes slid quickly across Tomiko's face as if to reassure himself that it was truly Hayato's daughter who was visiting his home. Then his eyes jumped to his mother and his father. His look gave the wordless order to leave the room.

Eda walked around the table and sat down facing Tomiko.

"What brings you to my house?" he asked, feeling his way. He affected a polite smile.

"You have a beautiful home," Tomiko answered evasively. "I have already looked at the pictures."

Eda turned his head and ran his eyes over the wall. "Yes, America, a beautiful country." He pulled the empty teacup toward him and filled it. "A rich country."

"I heard that you will soon be going back there."

"Yes," Eda drawled, slurpily gulping a sip of tea. "Yes, I'm going again. Business reasons, you might say."

Eda was not looking at Tomiko directly, but she was very acutely aware that he lost no opportunity to observe her out of the corner of his eye. She placed a small box of cookies—the little gift that was part of any visit—on the table and pushed it to one side.

"Thank you," Eda said.

Tomiko was in no hurry to state her request. She made use of the assurance granted her by her superior social station to first feel out how best to handle this man who was sitting across from her with his smooth smile and sharp eyes.

But Eda was not disconcerted by her serenity. With a quick, practiced gesture he lit a cigarette and put the match out with a snap of his fingers. After a brief hesitation—to make sure that the flame had died away—he threw the match on the floor. Tomiko noted that Eda no longer showed off the tattoos on his arms and chest as he used to. He wore a white shirt with long sleeves, which were buttoned at the cuffs. Even his collar was closed. She assumed that by now Eda was ashamed of his tattoos or no longer considered it proper to make a show of the blue, black, and red testament of his earlier life engraved on his skin.

"How is your honorable husband?" Eda asked, a hint of mockery in his voice.

"Very well," Tomiko hurried to reply.

"Does agreeable news reach you from America?"

Tomiko would not let his taunting questions disconcert her. Keeping her voice deliberately calm, she answered, "Oh, yes, very agreeable."

"When will he be returning?"

Tomiko was prepared for this question. "It has not been decided yet. I'm toying with the idea of taking a little trip to America myself," she added, as she had worked it out beforehand.

Unctuous and smug, Eda replied, "Oh, what interesting news. And it is this wish that has apparently directed the steps of the daughter of the house of Hayato to my modest home."

"Not a wish," Tomiko replied as casually as possible, "but simply the thought that it is not wrong for me to inquire into every possibility of traveling to America safely and in comfort."

Tomiko realized that while she spoke, Eda never took his eyes off her. A fleeting smile passed over his face, letting him appear disarmingly cheerful for a moment. "Ships leave for America from Kobe and Yokohama," he said, all business.

"I am aware of that. But I also heard that you are getting up a group voyage." Tomiko's nerves were stretched to the breaking point. She made an effort to appear indifferent. She kept her tone very factual, hoping in this way to solicit from Eda the information she was after.

Eda visibly enjoyed delaying his response to Tomiko's concern. He lit another cigarette and pushed the teapot toward Tomiko. "A little more tea, perhaps?" he asked.

"Thank you," Tomiko answered politely, filling her cup.

"Well, then, the matter of the group voyage," Eda began,

144

leaning back indolently. "It is a well-known fact that our compatriots who have been living in America for years are generally pretty well starved as far as women are concerned. They kill each other just to get the first turn in the whorehouse." Eda paused and awaited the effect of his words.

Tomiko sensed how he tried to wrest control of the conversation from her. The smiling cruelty in his eyes took her breath away. She remained silent and forced herself to swallow a sip of tea.

Eda was clearly satisfied with the effect his words had produced. He continued. "Naturally, in such a situation, a wife of one's own, in one's own bed, is like a million dollars in the bank. That is why I started the marriage-brokering business. A strange profession for a man who is still a bachelor, such as myself." He grinned and once again set his many laugh lines to wriggling. "And my success quite exceeds all expectations. Even now I have enlisted more women eager to get married than the ship's hold can contain. Many of them are spinsters—they won't find a husband at home anymore. The younger ones—they're the ones that give me trouble. They cling to their mothers' apron strings, and they cry their eyes out because they're afraid of the strange man they've only seen a photograph of. I only hope I can get all my women over the ocean in one piece."

Then Eda suddenly turned serious again, and once more his features took on their sly expression. "But such a journey, in the hold of a ship, is not suitable for Hayato's daughter. Is it that the honorable husband in America can't pay for a first-class passage? Or might Father Hayato be opposed to his daughter's leaving?"

Tomiko hurried to reply, "No, no," but she knew that she had hesitated a fraction of a second too long. Eda's lurking attentiveness had not missed her hesitation.

"But Father is well taken care of," he continued in a conversational tone. "The fisherman's daughter is at hand, so I've heard in town, and she is prepared to look after him day and night, should his daughter go to America." Eda sucked deeply at his cigarette, letting the smoke drift out through his nose. "But that is none of my business," he added, his tongue rolling the cigarette from one corner of his mouth to the other. "It's a full-time job finding enough women. Lately many men in America have asked me whether I couldn't get them one on the cheap. Oh, well, it's not cheap, the passage alone costs a pretty penny—in dollars. But these starved men are busting their britches. They're that crazy for women."

Eda nodded at Tomiko, and, with an insinuating wink, he added, "It's understandable, isn't it? Especially among seasonal laborers, who often toil like oxen for months, sixteen and eighteen hours a day, and then for weeks on end they're forced to sit around idle. They crack up pretty easy. I know all about it. In the course of time, thousands upon thousands of seasonal laborers passed through my hands. They owe their jobs on the farms to me. Recently I made a few inquiries to find out whether the honorable yōshi of the house of Hayato is among them. But I have not yet had the pleasure of running into him."

Tomiko felt the blood draining from her face and her hands began to tremble. "My husband is not a farm worker," she said, summoning all her strength to subdue the rage rising within her. "He practices a very interesting profession in San Francisco."

"Ah, so, in San Francisco . . . " drawled Eda.

 **20**

The letter of recommendation Fumiya had given Tomiko opened even the doors of the foreign ministry in Tokyo. The name of Ogasawara still had a magic ring. The ministerial official who saw Tomiko took her letter of recommendation with a civil gesture and read it through. "Oh, I had no idea about our engineer . . . so long ago . . . unfortunate accident . . . was married to an Ogasawara."

He sucked air through his teeth while one hand arranged the papers on his desk. "Please, have a seat. I remember him so well. At that time, as a young department head, I was in charge of his trip to America. Give me a moment to think. It's over thirty years ago. Oh . . . a great pity that he died so young. A very talented man. . . . And so you, too, are somehow related to the Ogasawaras?"

"Yes, my husband is the son of the engineer with whom you were acquainted."

147

"So that's how it is. Very interesting. If I understand you correctly, then, you are the engineer's daughter-in-law. I'm so pleased that you came to see me. I'm sure you never met your husband's father. Of course not—you were still a child, or not even born yet. But believe me, it was sensational—that time when your honorable husband's father traveled to America. A very great sensation. It was my first act of office to accompany him to the pier in Yokohama. Now I'm close to retirement. Oh, it pleases my soul to think back to the old times. . . . But please, do drink your tea. It will get cold otherwise. It is not a very good tea that they serve here in the foreign ministry. You'll have to forgive us. I'm certain the Ogasawara family serves a better tea. . . .

"As I was saying, your husband's father, our talented engineer, traveled on the Canadian Pacific Line. *Empress of China* was the name of the ship. First class, of course. We took that for granted, in those days. Today, alas, everything has changed, ever since so many kimin have been leaving for America. . . . Actually, I shouldn't even use the expression, but it's a fact that they are the dregs of our society. Nothing but young men who cannot make a go of it at home. Now they are sending for wives—by the boatload. It is inconceivable. It causes huge diplomatic problems. The American government has already lodged an official protest with us because we assign passports to these women. But we cannot help it—on paper they are married to one or another of our kimin over there. The Americans see only that all these women stream out of the ships' holds and look for their husbands at the pier while holding a photograph.

"Legally we can do nothing to stop the traffic, but we must be careful to make sure that friendly trade relations do not suffer because of it. Thanks to the merits of such men as your honorable husband's father, Japan has risen to the rank of the great powers. Truly a pity that he died so young. . . . How did it happen, actually?"

"A bridge collapse," Tomiko answered.

"Oh, yes, I remember. A major collapse—in Gifu Prefecture,

if I'm not mistaken. Truly a tragedy. . . . But what I meant to say . . . in those days, only the cream of the crop went to America, like the honorable father of your husband. To Europe, too, of course. They returned, and what they brought back was good for Japan: knowledge, technical skills, international connections. Today we must make a sharp distinction between the Japanese who are sent to America by our large corporations or the government departments and these kimin.

"I am not afraid to use the word—these people really are the dregs. Instead of remaining here, in their own country, where their roots are, they want to go to America and earn a lot of money quickly. Then they use the money to pay shady middlemen to bring women across the Pacific, and they get around the American immigration laws by entering into paper marriages with these women. Legally there is nothing we can do about it, and morally it is wrong, for what is to become of a blade of grass that has its roots in the divine Japanese soil? What becomes of it when it is cut off from its roots? I will tell you: In the alien country it becomes cattle fodder, a disgrace to all those in Japan who possess high cultural values and cultivated manners. . . .

"Would you believe, our consul in San Francisco tells us that more than once white people have pelted him with mud and empty tin cans because these confused whites cannot distinguish between the representative of our imperial government and one of the many kimins who loiter in the streets? Surely that is an insufferable situation for our country. If anything of the sort were to happen in Manchuria or China—I mean, our consul, and by extension our imperial government, to be so insulted— our armed forces stationed in those places would lose no time in making certain that there was no one left to throw mud and tin cans at an imperial Japanese consul. But in America, unfortunately, the situation is otherwise. There we cannot simply say, 'Stop your insults,' for those kimin are really there, thousands upon thousands of them, and they deserve no better than to be spattered with mud. . . .

"But we cannot bring back the kimin; for we ourselves do not

149

have enough space. What should we do with one hundred thousand kimin? When you come right down to it, we have to be glad that they are on the other side of the Pacific. And besides, they send dollars back to Japan. That is the only positive aspect of the kimin—that they send dollars. We use the currency to buy machinery and raw materials for our industries as well as weapons for our Greater Japanese Army. You see, there are two sides to everything, and even the dregs are useful. . . .

"But I am boring you with my stupid chatter. You cannot be interested in anything I am telling you. . . . As best I could make out from your letter of introduction, you live in the town where the Ogasawaras retired. Oh, it is wonderful to be born into a family with such a resounding name, or to marry into it. There the old culture is still alive, and the true nobility of spirit. People have not forgotten all the old values. Every gesture of the hands, every inclination of the head, each carefully uttered word—they all have a meaning. A person's entire bearing, inward as well as outward, is the expression of a cultural consciousness that has matured through the centuries. Between the internal and the external, genuine harmony exists to this day.

"Those of us who live here in Tokyo are consumed by the daily administrative work in the service of our people. We do not even have time to take an hour a day to sit in a beautiful garden and take joy in contemplating moss-covered rocks. The power of meditation is broken by the gears of the modern state. We exhaust ourselves in intrigues. Envy, greed, the thirst for glory lurk everywhere. . . . When I resign from active government service, which will be soon, I will devote myself to the contemplative life. I intend to breed goldfish. All I lack is a pond. I have always been fascinated by goldfish. Because of their infinite richness of color and patterns. . . . Is there anyone in your family who cultivates goldfish?"

"No," Tomiko said civilly.

"Their special attraction is that they live such a very long time. I specialize in calico goldfish; they are particularly beautiful when the sun shines through the leaves and dapples the surface with flickering spots of light. Then, when the calico goldfish plow the water with their powerful thrusts, their particular markings allow them to blend with the light patterns on the rippled surface of the pond. . . .

"But the Ogasawaras used to be famous for breeding goldfish. They introduced these noble fish from the old China to Japan and elevated their cultivation to an aristocratic occupation. Later, goldfish degenerated into pets for the masses—most regrettable. On the other hand, this craze allowed goldfish to become affordable. . . . Forgive me for telling you so much, but the name of Ogasawara has inspired me and suggested to me that I should ask you whether there might not be someone within your large family who still cultivates goldfish."

"That may well be," Tomiko replied. "But unfortunately I do not know."

"Oh, that is too bad. You are still young, and perhaps that is why you are not interested in goldfish. You really should be, though. What is more refreshing in the whole world than a still pond in which handsome goldfish swim? Believe me, though I am an old man compared to you, sometimes it is a good thing for today's young people to learn the eternal values. . . . But I see I have wandered from the original purpose of your visit again. What is the occasion of your coming to see me?"

Summoning up her courage, Tomiko said, "I wanted to ask you if I can obtain a passport to travel to America."

"A passport? Of course you can obtain a passport. An Ogasawara can always obtain a passport. When were you and your honorable husband planning to leave?"

"The date is still open," Tomiko countered evasively.

"Ah, America . . . it is a large country. There is much to be seen there. A beautiful country. I assume you wish to accompany your husband to New York and to Washington. I will give you the address of our ambassador there. Should you run into any problems, you need only turn to him. When you get to Washington, don't forget to look at the Japanese cherry trees decorating the shores of the Potomac. They are a symbol of our own goodwill in dealing with the kimin problem. In future we will have to make sharper distinctions between the decent Japanese, who go to America as agents of our respected corporations or as representatives of our government, and these kimin who look for work there because here at home they are too poor or too stupid to amount to anything. In America they are not ashamed to perform the most menial chores for the whites. Truly a disgrace to our empire. What right-thinking Japanese would ever get the idea just to pack up and go to America on his own to do the whites' dirty work?

"You must forgive me—I keep returning to this tiresome problem. If you go by way of San Francisco—actually a handsome city—you will probably be shocked by the number of kimin there. Unwashed, dirty creatures, that's what they are. A disgrace to our empire. If you will bring me a confirmation from the bank, I will make certain that you and your honorable husband receive your passports within three weeks."

"I need only one passport, for myself. My husband is already in San Francisco."

"Which concern does he work for?"

Tomiko had been expecting this dangerous question. "None," she said as nonchalantly as possible. "I wish to visit my husband."

"I understand . . . your husband is in America to pursue his studies. You must forgive my not having understood by myself. The Ogasawaras can afford it. At first, when you mentioned a passport, I thought that it was strange that you put the request personally. . . . But if it is to be a surprise for the gentleman, your husband, then I do understand. I was young once myself.

"For the members of Japanese firms abroad, you know, it's quite a different matter. The parent firm here in Japan takes care of obtaining the passport for the wife as well and buys her passage. In those cases only, the passport and the photographs pertaining to it pass across my desk. It is all very impersonal. It is rare that such a high-ranking visitor as yourself personally comes to my modest office. . . . If I may give you a piece of advice, book passage on the *President McKinley*. It is a large ship and is famous for its excellent first-class cabins. You will find the journey very pleasant. Please let me know the date when you will need a passport. I am honored that I can be of service to you. Since your honorable husband is already living in America, you do not require a bank confirmation—I forgot to mention that—about the financial affidavit for your stay in America. But don't forget the marriage certificate. . . . The Bureau of Families in your jurisdiction will be glad to issue it to you. I'm sorry I must insist on these formalities, but the conditions are very strict. The American officials simply do not let you in unless you can prove that you are the wife. . . .

"Well, then, it was a great honor to have been allowed to receive an Ogasawara in my office. Please do not think me forward if I close with a request: should you learn that anyone in your family still breeds goldfish . . . remember: calico goldfish, they are what I am interested in."

 21

Tomiko had stopped sewing. Nor did she look for new ways to earn money. Often she spent hours in the front room, sitting stiff and motionless while Rin worked in the kitchen or took care of her vegetable garden. The large new kimono chest made of the best kiri wood stood in the front room, taking up a whole wall. Since Nagayuki had sent money again, there was no other space for the many kimonos her father had added to his previous purchases for himself and Tomiko.

"Wouldn't a normal kimono chest of poplar wood do?" Tomiko asked.

"Only kiri wood effectively protects the silk kimonos against moths and keeps away humidity in the summer," Father pronounced.

"You look pale," he said later, laying his hand on Tomiko's shoulder in concern. "What a good thing that Rin is in the house now to relieve you of the housework."

His hair had grown completely white without losing its fullness. His eyebrows were more bushy than ever. But his skin had remained smooth and showed no signs of age. The white of his hair further brought out the freshness of his complexion.

"It is not well that you sleep in the front room and are disturbed every morning," her father continued. "I shall tell Rin to move downstairs. Upstairs you will be better able to rest."

Since Nagayuki's last remittance, Hayato always had a rickshaw call for him at home whenever he went into town. It was Michi's greatest joy to go with him in the rickshaw, and Father Hayato liked to have her along. "This afternoon I am going to the Friends of Noh, and I'm taking Michi with me," Father announced. He was speaking about some special anniversary of the establishment of the Noh Society, but Tomiko paid little attention.

Later she learned from Michi's lively description that a large banquet had been held. Michi told her mother that she had been the only child present. At the end, everyone had come to thank her and Grandfather.

Father Hayato softly stroked Michi's hair. "She was very well behaved. She is not a little child anymore."

Then Michi brought home the news that a beautiful new stone lantern had been erected at the Omiya shrine. "This high," Michi explained, raising her little arms. But they would not go high enough; she jumped with both feet, her arms stretched up. "This high!" she cried joyously. She spent a whole hour painting the stone lantern on a piece of paper. "That's you over here," she said to Father Hayato, pointing to a gigantic creature with long arms standing next to the lantern. "And this is me," she said, drawing a circle with two legs.

Father took her small, clumsy hand, which was still clutching the charcoal. "Do you know what it says on the pedestal of the lantern?" he asked softly.

"Hayato is what it says!" Michi crowed at the top of her lungs.

"Come, I'll show you how to write that." He guided her little hand and the charcoal stick across the paper to draw the two ideograms that formed the named Hayato. "That says Hayato," he repeated, pointing with one finger. "And that is what it says on the pedestal of the lantern. There the gods will read my name."

Michi, big-eyed, stared at him in admiration.

In this way Tomiko learned that her father had donated a new stone lantern to the Omiya shrine. In this way he had once more engraved his name in the public consciousness. His name, chiseled into the pedestal, gave proof that Father Hayato had reason to be grateful to the gods. Everyone who walked the long path from the torii to the main building of the Omiya shrine could and must see this stone lantern, which stood at a curve in the path.

Very many people had been there, Michi related, still very excited, when the stone lantern was dedicated. Grandfather had promised to take her there at night, when he would light the lantern. Now only a sakaki branch lay where the light was supposed to burn. She had put the branch there herself, Michi said with childish gravity, all by herself, while Grandfather held her up. "He can hold me very high," she said, looking at Gen. "Much higher than you."

At thirteen, Gen was unusually strong. He had inherited his powerful physique and his large, round eyes from Rin. But his features were very like those of Father Hayato. He had the same oval head and the same straight nose and high forehead. When he smiled, it was as if one were looking at Father Hayato's smile. Even strangers became aware of the astonishing resemblance when they saw Father Hayato and Gen together.

When Tomiko moved into the upstairs room and Rin carried her mattress downstairs, Gen was in no hurry to gather up his things and take them down. "I want to be allowed to stay here," he said to Tomiko softly and shyly.

Tomiko was pleased at his request and agreed to it. Michi,

who, according to Father Hayato's wish, was to move upstairs with Tomiko, resisted vigorously and begged to go on sleeping in the back room with him.

"No," Father Hayato said, determined. "You may spend the day with me, but at night you must go upstairs."

Although Michi did not pout in Father Hayato's presence, she sulked for a long time because Tomiko put her to bed in the upper room. During the night Tomiko often heard her grind her teeth in her sleep.

Gen's physical strength and agility expressed themselves in his enthusiasm for judo. Father Hayato welcomed Gen's attachment to the old Japanese form of fighting, for, as he said, "Judo strengthens the spirit as well as the body." Father Hayato enjoyed telling of earlier sumurai who with their bare hands overpowered an enemy armed with a sword.

Gen was to become familiar with all the great names of samurai heroes who had been so exceedingly superior to their opponents in battle that they had been able to discard their own swords. Without a weapon in hand and without any armor, they went into battle against a fully protected, fully armed enemy. They moved so cleverly that the enemy's sword lunges never touched them. They waited until their opponent, propelled by the force of his own thrust into the void, advanced too far forward by a handsbreadth. Then they grabbed him and in a flash flung him to the ground. With the sword, which they wrested from his hand, they separated the enemy's head from his trunk.

"A well-deserved end for a bad fighter," Father Hayato exclaimed. "Those were real samurai still. Fearlessly they looked their opponent in the eyes and conquered him."

Father Hayato never tired of explaining to Gen that in judo, as in life, it was a matter of never allowing one's opponent to dictate one's actions. Otherwise one might unwittingly fall into a trap and be bested.

"Constant alertness, loyalty, and contempt for death are the

157

virtues of the samurai," he explained to Gen. "Whoever has wholly absorbed this deep wisdom and has become totally wedded to it finds himself on the road to becoming a true samurai. You are on this road, because you are a good judo fighter."

When they were alone, he said to Tomiko, "Someday this boy will win back all our family possessions if Nagayuki cannot manage it."

Gen always listened in silence when Father Hayato spoke to him, but his large, melancholy eyes looked indifferent. But it was not that he was disinterested in judo. He was a zestful judo fighter and proud of his achievements in this field. It was only the stories of the samurai that held no attraction for him. He refused even to remember the names of the heroes.

When Gen found Tomiko alone at home, he proudly showed her his championship certificate. Tomiko was sitting in the upper room, her eyes vacant, her hands folded idly in her lap. She looked through the wide-open shoji screens down into the street, as she did every day, endlessly waiting for the ticket which would have to arrive soon from Nagayuki.

"You are so sad," Gen said. "Aren't you glad I won the judo belt?"

"Yes, of course. I'm glad for you."

"I'm the best in my class, and I even won over the best in the eighth and the ninth grade."

"You're very big and strong."

Gen showed her his newly won judo belt. "But you're not even looking at it."

"Yes, I am. It's a third-level belt. Usually you have to be fifteen before you can win it."

"That's what the teacher said, too. He even thought that now I can get admitted to the judo club in town. Do you think I should join?"

"Perhaps it's a good idea."

"Then I could practice twice a week at the Eda Hall. Do you know the Eda Hall?"

"I've passed it, yes."

"You should go inside one day. It's wild! If there's a contest and I'm competing, will you come?"

"Yes, I'll come."

After her return from Tokyo, Tomiko had immediately called on Fumiya to report about her interview in the foreign ministry. "Do you know what a kimin is?" she asked Fumiya.

"No," Fumiya answered. "I've never heard the word."

Gen was looking at Tomiko with quiet concentration. "You're so sad again," he said softly.

When Tomiko did not reply, he went to the wooden box where he proudly kept his many seashells and snail casings. Their number and variety had increased considerably over the years. Rin's father still brought him any choice specimens he found in his net when he went trawling. But Gen himself had gathered many of the most attractive pieces himself on the beach or had brought them up from the ocean floor. Every time he came home with a particularly beautiful example of a large, oddly horned kind of snail or one of the plate-sized, flat abalone shells, its inner surface iridescent with scarlet and glowing nacre, he showed it to Tomiko.

Now she heard him at her back, emptying the box completely. Finally there was a silence, and Gen came to her side quietly. He was holding an ivory-colored cowrie, smooth-shelled, cool, and just big enough to be enfolded in both hands. Gen pressed the shell close to Tomiko's ear.

"Can you hear the ocean roaring?" he asked.

"Yes," said Tomiko and wept.

 **22**

Fumiya proposed abandoning all thought of America. Instead, she said to Tomiko, Nagayuki should return home. "As soon as possible. It serves no good purpose, it will lead to nothing, for him to stay in America any longer."

Tomiko did not speak for a long time. This possibility had never occurred to her. When Fumiya continued, saying, "Anyway, who says that Nagayuki must return dressed in brocade?" Tomiko nodded.

But immediately she replied, "Father—"

Fumiya shook her head vehemently. "You'll simply go to Tokyo. With Nagayuki and Michi. In the big city, Nagayuki, with his Todai diploma, will start anew."

"But Father—" Tomiko repeated.

"Nagayuki doesn't even have to come to Himari. You'll take Michi to Tokyo. You'll meet Nagayuki there."

Tomiko needed time to grow used to this new idea. Through all the recent years, her thoughts had been directed exclusively to America and the idea that somehow she must go there, at some time. All the plans she had harbored and hedged were directed to this single goal. Even if all that was left of her plans now were ashes—Tomiko's thoughts had not yet progressed so far as to accept the possibility that Nagayuki could be called back. Now Fumiya faced her with this new, outrageous idea. It sounded so simple. Fumiya described Tomiko's way with such matter-of-factness that Tomiko wondered why she herself had not thought of it before.

"If you should actually be able to go to America, nothing awaits you but uncertainty," Fumiya said.

Tomiko knew that Fumiya was right. Perhaps she would not even be able to take Michi with her. Michi would be an obstacle if Tomiko had to look for work. She would have to work as a domestic servant—at best. For rich white people. No one would hire a maid with a child. So she would have to leave Michi behind, at home, or give up the idea of getting work in America. But if she had no work, she would be a burden to Nagayuki.

More and more frequently tears rose to Tomiko's eyes when, in town, she saw a man and a woman with a child Michi's age. Whether the father was carrying the child while the mother stood close by or whether the mother and father walked along the street, the child between them—every time the naturalness with which other people exhibited their family happiness stirred Tomiko to the depths. To avoid such images, she avoided going into town. But then she saw the images in her dreams. They showed her a father who looked like Nagayuki, with a little girl who crowed with joy like Michi and could not be controlled. The father swung the child upward and let her fly through the air for a little. With a sure hand, he caught her again. In her dreams, she herself stood close by and was not afraid.

Fumiya was inexorable. "You must stop surrendering to dreams that are nothing but self-deception. If you go to America, you stop being the daughter of Hayato and become a cheap pair of hands. If you take Michi with you, you'll turn her into a kimin child. Who knows, white children might beat her. Where do you intend leaving her when you have to go out to earn money? What school will she attend one day? Do you want to send her to a school where the children of other Japanese go? Maybe even the children of Japanese who are spending time in America quite officially, on a mission for the imperial government or as agents for a Japanese firm? Surely they are the most cruel of all, wanting to have nothing to do with the kimin and their children because they are the dregs of society."

Tomiko wished she could contradict Fumiya and shout that Fumiya was exaggerating. She wanted to cling to Nagayuki's last letter, in which he had written that he was doing better now and had found more regular work.

"What kind of work?" Fumiya asked in a tone that almost anticipated the answer. "Why doesn't Nagayuki write exactly what he does? How he lives? Where he works and used to work?"

Tomiko was forced to admit that Nagayuki had never given precise details about his daily life. His letters never contained descriptions of his work. He never wrote how much he earned; he just sent money, instead. The sums always appeared huge to Tomiko, so that she imagined that the sources from which the dollars flowed spurted richly. This fantasy fed her dreams, for she could never think of Nagayuki other than surrounded by blossoming apricot trees, under a sky of luminous blue, or against a background of surf-washed, rocky shores above which, in the distance, white glaciers glittered. Even if long ago Fumiya had sown doubts in her and these doubts had at times sprouted into anxious visions, her hope that everything really was as she dreamed continued to flicker.

"It is too late," Tomiko said softly. "Too late for everything."

"No." Fumiya flared up. "It is not too late. Nagayuki will find a job in Tokyo—if only as a teacher . . . to start with," she quickly added when she saw that Tomiko was shaking her head in

162

disapproval. "I know that is not the future you have in mind and the kind that used to be open to Nagayuki—at the time he graduated from Todai. In those days the biggest firms fought over him. Now those doors are closed. But a teacher of languages. . . ."

Tomiko realized how fully Fumiya had already thought out every possibility still open to Nagayuki. There was no hope of joining any of the better firms. They would ask Nagayuki where he had worked in America, what his position and his job had been. No one wants to hire a returned farmhand or a day laborer who slaved in a fish cannery. No one wants to hire a onetime kimin—even if he comes with a Todai diploma and even if he was first in his class.

It no longer counts. Not now, not five years later.

The possibility that remained, then, was to earn money by teaching languages.

"I am certain that by now Nagayuki speaks English as well as the best of them," Fumiya said. "It is not a bad thing for him to be a language teacher in Tokyo. Language teachers are in great demand."

Fumiya did all she could to sweep Tomiko along. She was animated as she described how Nagayuki would have to work as a language teacher only long enough to make a new beginning in Tokyo. The time would come when he could make use of the connections with important people he would forge, and the confidence he would earn, to build up something of his own. Perhaps a legal office or some kind of consulting firm where he could make use of his American experiences.

"After all," said Fumiya, "the greatest difficulty the Japanese encounter is that they do not understand the Western mentality. They do not know how to behave when they have to deal with white people. That is why misunderstandings keep occurring when they could have been avoided. Nagayuki could help to reduce them. He has what it takes."

It was hard for Tomiko to resist the tidal wave of new hopes Fumiya unleashed, carrying her thoughts away into new

163

dreams. But when she realized that all the plans Fumiya had so zealously developed depended on whether it would be possible to persuade Nagayuki to return quickly, even without brocade, she said to Fumiya, "You don't know Nagayuki."

Fumiya laughed. "He is my son . . . don't forget."

Tomiko's expression remained grave. She bowed slightly. "Forgive me," she said. "I didn't mean it that way. But Nagayuki has changed since he stopped being your son. My father changed him."

The smile vanished from Fumiya's features. She looked at Tomiko with an expression of almost awesome grief. Then she closed her eyes and listened without a word while Tomiko, first hesitantly then with increasing warmth told how, under Father's instruction, Nagayuki had to learn all the techniques which—as Father put it—would be useful to him someday, should he be able to defend his honor only by death. For months Father practiced with him daily and showed him how to hold the dagger; how far the handle must be wrapped in the white cloth, the sequence in which the thrusts were to be executed, and how concentrated breath could hold back the flow of blood and at the same time collect enough strength so that one's hands would not fail before the last stab through one's own throat had been made.

Finally Father set the day of the solemn ceremony when the old Hayato dagger was to be handed down to Nagayuki, the new bearer of the Hayato name. "From now on," Father said as he presented the dagger, "this dagger shall accompany you always. Its image shall be in your heart, so that its blade will serve to protect the honor of the name of Hayato."

Tomiko was allowed to stand in the background to attend the ceremony. She saw Nagayuki's pale, serious face and his eyes, while he made an effort not to look frightened. She could not see Father's face. He sat in front of Nagayuki, very upright, his head raised solemnly, but she felt that her father's eyes were resting lovingly on Nagayuki. Father Hayato wore a pure white garment, and Nagayuki, too, was dressed wholly in white, as tradition demanded. Both sat on a white cloth—the blood-collecting cloth, which would keep the spatters of blood from the floor. On a silken pillow between them lay the dagger. Tomiko could see clearly the wavy pattern etched into the handle. Although at the time she, too, had been gripped by the solemnity of the occasion and made a genuine effort to feel pride in the moment, she vaguely suspected that with this ceremony something in Nagayuki was irrevocably broken—something she would come to miss later on. She looked at her mother, to see if she shared her feelings, but her mother's face was motionless and closed.

Father said to Nagayuki, "The calm acceptance of transitoriness and death leads you to the threshold of manhood. In the form of this dagger, the mature realization unfolds to you that a great name is also a great responsibility. Only he who is prepared to give his life for the name can preserve it from filth and degradation."

During his time at Todai, Nagayuki had the dagger in Tokyo. He kept it in a rectangular box of kiri wood, and Tomiko was not allowed to touch it. Nagayuki never raised its lid either, but once Tomiko surprised him when he had taken the dagger out after all and was holding it in a strangely stiff grip. When Nagayuki realized that Tomiko had entered the room, he put the dagger away without a word and closed the lid of the box. All that day he did not speak, and in the evening he said abruptly, "If I do not graduate at the top of my class, I will die."

That had been during his last year at the university. As his final exams moved closer, Nagayuki cried out in his sleep more and more frequently. Tomiko tried to calm him, and she helped him as best she could to prepare for his exams. Then Nagayuki fell ill, and for three days he was unable to attend the lectures. As Tomiko bent over his bed and laid a cooling compress on his forehead, he said softly, "I'm afraid of dying."

For a long time, Fumiya remained motionless, her eyes closed.

She seemed to be listening to the sound of Nagayuki's voice, which Tomiko had retrieved from a lost time. Then she opened her eyes and stared silently into the void.

"You're trying to tell me that Nagayuki will not come back from America?" she asked at last.

"Not as long as he thinks of himself as a failure."

"Even if I were to write him?"

"Not even then," Tomiko replied. "Nagayuki will not come back as long as he is a failure. Before he left, Father Hayato made him promise. Sooner than break his promise, Nagayuki will die."

"If Nagayuki returned without brocade, that would be proof of the greatest inner strength," Fumiya observed.

But Tomiko was no longer listening to what Fumiya was saying. Her gaze was rigid. "I must go to him. I must. He must send me a steamship ticket. Not money anymore. Just the ticket," she murmured.

Once more Fumiya tried to change Tomiko's mind. "Do you really expect that with your puny help Nagayuki could prepare himself in America for an honorable return?"

When Tomiko did not speak, Fumiya added softly, "I think then there will be no return at all."

 **23**

When the first bell of the new clock of the Kannon temple rang out and the dark, heavy sound traveled over the town and the bay of Himari, Tomiko closed her eyes. Slowly the sound ebbed away, carried on the air and tossed back by the hills behind the town. It took a long time before the second bell sounded, and then, after a pause that encompassed the time of a dream, the third bell, already almost familiar, like an earlier time, when each night the old bell of the Kannon temple had poured its dull sound over the city at regular intervals.

When she was a little girl, Tomiko never dared to go close to the large old gong when the monk in his flowing black garment marched to the low pagoda under whose curved roof the large, heavy mass of poured bronze hung. Only after Nagayuki had joined the Hayato household and she felt braver in his presence than she did alone, did she go with him to the Kannon temple.

There they waited until it was the hour for the daily striking of the gong.

From a respectful distance they watched as the monk stepped on the wooden pedestal and with measured steps approached the heavy wooden beam. This beam was suspended on two thick slings of rope and loomed far out between the pillars of the bell pagoda. After a ceremonial bow, the monk first placed his hand on the beam as if to test how easy or hard it would be to move. Then he grasped it firmly in both hands and gave it its first swing, in an arc that was still far from touching the side of the gong. The gong hung heavy and silent from the strutted and braced rafters of the pagoda's roof, its bottom edge almost touching the dais where the monk stood. But then the monk pulled the beam so far back that the ropes groaned, and in swinging it forward, he gave it an additional push. The powerful beam shot forward, first with a slight downswing, then rising again and, with a boom, it struck the side of the gong. If you were standing close by, you could hear another sound escaping from the wooden beam as it bounded back. But this sound died down quickly, and only the peal of the big bell filled the air. It penetrated deep into the bowels and made your eyes ache. All other sounds ceased for the length of a breath under the brunt of this wave of noise. Then the sound lessened, and slowly the sea of heavy vibrations parted to release anew the familiar high screechings of the many cicadas or the song of the birds. The monk waited until the sound of the bell had died down enough to be overpowered by the crunch of gravel on the path or the distant shout of a rickshaw driver. Only then did he raise his arms again, circle the beam, pull it back with all his strength, and let it dash against the gong for the second peal.

Each time the powerful sound arose, Tomiko clung tight to Nagayuki, and he readily returned the pressure of her body. In the course of the years, as the desire for touch grew in Tomiko, the effects of the samurai tales which Father Hayato bestowed on Nagayuki became ever more pronounced. They dammed up the tenderness inherent in the boy.

"First of all, a samurai destroys within himself any feeling for women," the father had often enough admonished Nagayuki. He had also prepared Tomiko for her part as a wife. "Women's feelings are sticky threads, winding themselves around the arm of the samurai. If he gives in, he will never be free and cannot muster up the courage to confront life's more important tasks."

Tomiko knew that for too long she had been unresisting in accepting the role her father had assigned her. She had never really rebelled against it, had never consciously tried to loosen Nagayuki's ties to their father. She had never dared to feed the tender feelings sprouting in Nagayuki to the extent that Nagayuki would become hers altogether.

"The samurai grows in the negation of any attachment to women."

But Tomiko thought she had recognized that Nagayuki's innermost being was shaped by the need for tenderness. She also knew that she alone was the object of his tenderness. Nagayuki never expressed his special affection for her as clearly as he did during the years in Tokyo, where he found his way back to the warm, seeking caresses she had felt for the first time at the moss-covered edge of the hot spring between the rocks at the back of the Hayato estate. Although the dagger, which embodied the constant nearness of death in which a samurai was to live, rested in a corner of the bedroom, and although Nagayuki often threw himself with excessive zeal into studying the eleven-volume code of the samurai, Himari was so strangely distant while they lived in Tokyo that at moments Tomiko forgot the power of her father's influence over Nagayuki.

Since Nagayuki had gone to America alone in spite of her entreaties, because that was what Father Hayato had demanded of him, Tomiko felt that she had failed. She had been unable to guide him back to the core of his nature, which was totally opposed to the grim spirit of the samurai. She had tried to influence him a little, but she had been too quick to console herself with the thought that the father would never quite succeed in hollowing out Nagayuki and filling him with iron.

169

Tomiko had overestimated the power of her feelings and recognized too late the limits of her capacities.

The night under the mosquito netting, Father Hayato needed to ask Nagayuki just once whether he was prepared to carry out the task assigned him. The fear of appearing a coward in Father Hayato's eyes had driven Nagayuki to America.

Even though Fumiya had said to him in a gentle but urgent voice, "The greatest cowardice is to obey blindly."

That had been as they stood at the Yasukuni shrine in Tokyo, on the fifth anniversary of the death of Nagayuki's two older brothers. Fumiya had come to Tokyo to take part in the tribute to the war dead which the Tenno personally celebrated twice a year at the Yasukuni shrine. Crowded in with a mass of people, they walked up the long ramp. Pine branches stretched over the path on the right and the left. In wide serpentines the way led up to a broad, gravel-covered space, where the main shrine was visible behind a pillared porch. There, surrounded by pines waving in the autumn wind, the people stood closely ranked. When the Tenno appeared to perform the ritual in the interior of the shrine, the people lowered their heads, and even the weeping of the mothers was stilled. Only Fumiya remained standing upright, looking at the curving roof of the shrine, under whose protection lived the souls of the war dead. Many women near her and all over the area murmured the names of their fallen husbands or sons and thanked them for the sacrifice which had brought victory to their country.

Later, when the crowd had scattered, Fumiya stepped closer to the shrine. She walked among the people who still remained, alone or in little clumps, sunk in prayer on the broad plaza. She made a delicate figure dressed in black, who did not yet seem to feel the weight of the years on her shoulders. Then she stood before the steps over which, as someone observed in awe, barely an hour ago the Tenno had walked into the shrine's interior.

"None of those who are being honored here brought the sacrifice out of their own free choice—though many of them

170

died gladly because they had been persuaded that their death was necessary for the honor of their country."

When Tomiko heard these words, in this place, it seemed to her that the wind was holding its breath. The trees did not rustle; the rafters inside the shrine did not creak.

"There is only one kind of death," Fumiya said. Only as she walked down the long ramp with Tomiko and Nagayuki did the wind ruffle the treetops again.

Tomiko wondered whether at that time, at the Yasukuni shrine in Tokyo, Fumiya already suspected the extent to which Nagayuki was under Father Hayato's spell. Probably not, or she would have spoken to him even more urgently and plainly.

After Tomiko had written to Nagayuki to send her a steamship ticket, she felt more relieved. "Please send it to me by registered mail," she had added at the end of the letter in which she had reported, keeping the tone as cheerful and light as possible, that Michi and father continued well and how happy she was at the thought of joining him in America soon. She avoided any word that might betray the true situation in which she found herself.

When eight weeks had passed and Tomiko could expect Nagayuki's answer to arrive any day, she did not leave the house for even a moment. Most of the time she sat in the upper room, close to the wide-open shoji screen, gazing across the front yard to the street, where the mailman came by twice a day. She took care not to betray her excitement when he stopped before the house, took letters out of his pouch, and entered the garden. Then she hastened down the steep ladder to see if a letter from Nagayuki, addressed to her, was among them. She wanted to make very sure that Nagayuki's letter would be placed in her own hand.

One night she started up from a dream in which she had clearly seen the mailman, holding a particularly thick letter from America, bowing at the door and calling to ask whether anyone was at home. Only the father was home, and he answered the door. He put out his hand for the letter. Behind him, in the tokonoma recess, the Nabeshima vase glowed strangely, as if from within, and the door of the kimono chest of precious kiri wood could no longer be closed because too many kimonos welled out of the drawers. Without a word Father Hayato took receipt of the letter. Then, with a quiet smile, he slit open the envelope and pulled out the steamship ticket. He scrutinized it at length, turned it this way and that, read the name, and finally tore it in half with a firm hand.

 **24**

The consecration of the bell provided the town with a subject of conversation for a long time. The priest of the Kannon temple had been collecting for a new bell in Himari for years, but the amount he had laid by had been far from sufficient.

It was Eda who made an unexpectedly lavish donation from the money he had earned in America and thus made possible the acquisition of the large bell. The townspeople used to speak of Eda as the son of the old dockworker; then he was called Judo Hall Eda; now the people spoke of him as Lord Eda, who had given the money for the bell.

This act had raised Eda almost to the rank of the local dignitaries of Himari. In accordance with this honor, Eda dressed in an increasingly middle-class way. He wore tightly tailored Western suits of dark cloth, and even on the hottest days he had on a shirt with a stiff collar and buttoned cuffs, so that even the townspeople, who generally had excellent memories,

173

hardly ever mentioned the fact that Eda's chest and arms were covered with tattoos.

Some of the town girls from the poorer families may well have had hopes that Eda would marry one of them. It was out of the question that he would be able to get a daughter from one of the better Himari families, for in spite of the donation of the bell, the people's memories were not quite that short. By now it was no longer a secret—even Rin no longer kept it from Father Hayato—that Eda had married Rin's youngest sister.

One day the priest of the Kannon temple had come to Rin's father just as he was about to unload his boat and hang the nets up to dry on poles in front of the house. "You are a good fisherman," the priest said, "and the Buddha on the lotus blossom grants you mercy. A very rich man wants to take your youngest daughter as his wife. He has charged me to ask you. Do you agree?"

Rin's father, who had never before been granted the honor of a personal conference with the priest of the Kannon temple— certainly not in his own home—could not utter a word in his confusion. He merely nodded and bowed deeply.

"Then come to see me at the temple an hour before sundown tomorrow," the priest said. "We'll settle everything there. Bring your daughter with you."

So Rin's youngest sister became Eda's wife, and Rin's father was given enough money by Eda to allow him to buy a motor for his own fishing skiff.

"That's why," Rin said repeatedly at dinner, and Father Hayato no longer protested when the name of Eda was mentioned in his presence, "that's why my little sister could become bell maiden."

In the days before the ceremony to consecrate the bell, no one could yet have any suspicion that it was Rin's sister of all people whom Eda would marry. That is why it seemed quite miraculous to Rin that her little sister, out of all the world—a girl who was

174

certainly nobody special—had been chosen by the priest of the Kannon temple to be first, after himself and the mayor, to ring the new bell. Quite secretly Rin had confided to Tomiko, "My sister—the youngest one—is going to be bell maiden for the consecration ceremony." Rin added in a whisper, "I'm sure she's still a maiden—my little sister—but I don't understand why the priest did not give preference to the mayor's granddaughter. She's the same age as my sister. Or someone in the families of the town councillors. They have daughters, too."

Rin simply could not take it in. "The Buddha on the lotus blossom cares for us poor fishermen. If it has to be the daughter of a fisherman, why my sister out of all the others?"

While Rin's sister sat on the dais for the consecration of the bell, Rin, with Gen and little Michi, pushed her way to the front row on the opposite side. The people said, "Here comes Rin, the older sister of the bell maiden. Let her pass."

From her seat Rin could look over the entire dais. First, of course, she saw her little sister, in a white kimono with large, bright flowers, sitting all the way at the front, in the most conspicuous place, between a lot of important men dressed in black. Even without the powder, her face would have been very white. The round red spots on both cheeks stood out brightly, surpassed only by the cherry-red of her lips.

Rin's little sister pursed her mouth in awareness of her responsibilities as a bell maiden. She stared straight ahead, her eyes lowered, and kept her hands pressed in her lap. She sat between the mayor and the judge. The shinto priest from the Omiya shrine had also come and was sitting in his blue-and-white robes between the black-clad town councillors.

Then Rin's eyes looked for Father Hayato, who had taken his place in the third row. She helped Michi and Gen to find him there. Michi waved, shouting loudly and jumping up and down, but Father Hayato's face was serious and solemn, and he paid no attention to Michi's shrieks. The people around them muttered to each other that the fat man behind the mayor was the representative of the prefectural government. The town councillors were examined one by one, to make sure all were present. When someone discovered the headmaster of the public school, he pointed him out to the others with an outstretched finger, as he did the head of the girls' school and the director of the secondary boys' school. All heads turned in the direction indicated, and everyone gave a satisfied nod.

All the other notables of the town had also been accommodated on the dais. Not far from Father Hayato sat the doctor, the owner of the newspaper, and the captain of Himari's only passenger boat, and of course the merchants with shops on the main street.

The large new bell was still shrouded with a white cloth. The priest of the Kannon temple stood by in his gleaming saffron Buddhist robes, which enfolded him in deep, flowing folds. His assistant remained in the background, trembling with barely suppressed expectation of the moment when he would be allowed to pull the cloth away from the bell. The mayor's speech publicly proclaimed the person to whom the town owed the gift of the new bell. It was also true, however, that during the last seven years many citizens had given considerable sums according to their ability and with an open hand so that the bell might be acquired. The priest of the Kannon temple was infinitely grateful to them all.

"None of us here in Himari is rich in these difficult times," the mayor said, "but our town has a brave son who has dared to cross the wide Pacific and has carried the name of our town of Himari beyond the hundred horizons. Dressed in brocade, he returned. I am speaking of Mr. Eda, whom all of us know because he has already given us the Judo Hall. Now, through an exceedingly generous donation, he has endowed the Kannon temple with the amount that was still lacking in the sum needed to acquire our bell."

The final words of the mayor's speech were almost drowned in the jubilation that broke out—the clapping, the shouting, the crowding and pushing. The mayor turned to look up at the dais. He made a sign to Eda to rise. Eda, who humbly sat in the very

176

last row, rose from his seat and bowed to all sides with a thin smile.

The people said, "That Eda—even though he brought back so much money from America and keeps going back to America to get more money . . . in his heart, Eda has remained humble."

"Eda proposed my little sister as bell maiden because he had it in mind to marry her all along," Rin repeated, excited. "That is how it was, isn't it?" she asked Tomiko.

"That probably was the reason," Tomiko answered gently, but inwardly she was disturbed, for Eda's ploy struck her with fear. By marrying Rin's youngest sister, he had become an immediate danger; as Rin's brother-in-law, he had one foot in the door of the Hayato home. She knew that he would come.

Father Hayato sat in the front room and in his deliberate, cool manner sipped his after-dinner cup of tea. Tomiko saw her father turn his head when, behind her, Eda's voice came from the open door. "Forgive the intrusion."

Without haste Father Hayato glanced toward the door. He betrayed no astonishment. Tomiko noticed that only his back straightened by a hair. When Eda's head appeared in the door opening, Father spoke the inevitable invitation to enter the house with cool dignity. More polite than custom required, Eda and his young wife remained standing before the two steps leading into the house and bowed deeply. Rin ran to the door and there, behind the sill, knelt on the tatami mats. She bowed and, as duty required, said to Eda that he surely had no need to take the trouble to come here.

"But it is my pleasure and honor to visit the older sister I have gained through my marriage," Eda answered with another bow.

With these words he laid his gift—a package wrapped in rice paper and tied with a red-and-white ribbon—on the doorsill. Then he stood waiting, his chalk-white suit and straw hat had both quite evidently been brought back from America. "Only a little something," he added, "for I am well aware that in this house an exquisite taste reigns which I could never achieve."

When Tomiko looked at her father, she could tell from the expression on his face that he did not receive Eda's words unfavorably.

Eda combined his words with a submissive posture. He spoke over Rin's head while she went on kneeling at the doorsill and exchanging covert gestures with her sister who stood outside, in the garden, invisible to Tomiko. Eda had his arms slightly at an angle, and one hand grasped the fingers of the other, as if he were chilly in the damp July heat. He held his head pushed far forward, and with each word his torso rocked to demonstrate his devotion. But behind the gesture and behind the sharply observing glance of his ever-smiling eyes, Tomiko recognized his sly calculations.

"When I recently had the pleasure of visiting the honorable son of the house of Hayato in San Francisco, our conversation turned on this very topic of taste," Eda said. He brought the sentence to a close without dropping his voice. Tomiko felt a cold shiver run down her spine.

"Oh," Father Hayato replied, looking expectantly at Eda. "You visited my son? You really did?"

"I had a hard time locating him."

"Tomiko, did you hear? Mr. Eda has news from America." Beaming with joy, Father turned to Tomiko. It was the first time he had spoken of "Mr. Eda."

Eda bowed and gave full play to his laugh lines. "The honorable daughter of the house of Hayato had the goodness some time ago to call my attention in passing to the fact that the honorable son of the house is at present spending time in San Francisco." The half-moon-shaped folds that framed Eda's lips were joined by crows' feet at the corners of his eyes, letting his features appear especially cheerful.

Tomiko sensed her whole body stiffen in fear. She looked at her father in the hope that he would understand the warning in her eyes, but Hayato was in good spirits and smiled happily. The poison of Eda's politeness had already infected him.

"Come closer," Father invited Eda, but Eda replied, without

leaving his place outside the door, "I am ashamed that we came so suddenly, without announcing ourselves. I do not wish to take further advantage of your time."

"No, really," Father insisted. "Come in and sit down."

"My wife and I are very ashamed," Eda protested with another deep bow, "and not at all prepared to respond to such an honorable invitation. Most assuredly we do not wish to disturb you."

"No, no, that is not the case at all," Father repeated his invitation for the third time. "Come in and tell me about my son."

"Bring some tea," he ordered, turning to Rin.

It was then that Eda simply stated that Nagayuki was well and sent him regards.

 **25**

Father Hayato had moved his bonsai trees behind the house. Through the open windows and doors Tomiko could hear him initiating Gen into the methods by which he dwarfed newly planted young trees. Michi was outside with them, eagerly fetching wire, newspaper, a brush, and sand, and taking them back again. The father patiently explained to Gen which branches were to be lopped in order to breed a wind-tousled bonsai and which ones to achieve a very smoothly grown trunk.

Tomiko heard him pinching off pieces of wire with the cutters. She could tell from his words that her father was winding the stiff wire around a still-pliable branch from which he had stripped all buds and twigs, to bend it permanently in the desired direction. Michi kept interrupting with her chatter. Gen was apparently listening in silence. When the father ordered him to remove excess twigs from a branch he intended to bend, the faltering snap of the scissors told Tomiko that Gen was now handling them.

"Why are bonsai trees beautiful?" Gen asked.

Father Hayato remained silent so long that Tomiko was already instinctively smiling, for she actually had a physical sensation of his bewilderment through the walls.

"Just as the sound of the drops that fall from the bamboo pipe at the well always hold an echo of the rushing waterfall in the mountains for the practiced ear, so a single bonsai tree embodies the breath of all the forests," Father Hayato finally said. And to Gen he issued an order: "Sit down."

While various sounds indicated the progress of his work on the bonsai trees, he spoke of the objective stillness created by the conscious striving for shape. Like human beings, the objects of nature were also capable of unlimited development, which gave to life as a whole its deeper meaning. The necessary basis for arriving at the higher stages of development, however, was the performance of daily observances.

"You are familiar with these ideas from your devotion to judo," Father Hayato said to Gen. "You must practice and exercise daily to attain mastery, to which you have come so close at such an early age. Why, then, do you practice?"

"Because I enjoy it?"

"That is not enough. Joy is gained only from total mastery of the self. When the self has overcome the uncontrolled movements of the body, fear vanishes, and you will be able to vanquish any opponent. Even a net that is cast over you in battle cannot catch you because your spirit is free."

"But I still don't know why bonsai trees are beautiful," Gen said with a perplexity that could not be ignored.

"Because they have become perfect. This perfection cannot be comprehended through questions but only through observation. By observation you penetrate to the roots of being. Do you see this bonsai tree over there, which is already almost perfect? Sit here and observe it for an hour without moving."

A little later, Father Hayato, holding Michi by the hand,

181

returned to the front room. There he took up his usual place while Rin ran at once to prepare hot water for tea.

"Why does Gen have to sit out there?" asked Michi in her bright voice, snuggling up to her grandfather.

"You're too young to understand. He is about to become a man."

Soon she'll be going to school, Tomiko thought as she watched Michi sitting close to Father Hayato. We haven't had her picture taken in a long time. Nagayuki would be happy to see how like his her features are.

Often in the evenings Tomiko sat for a long time in the upper room at Michi's bedside after she had put the child to bed and told her stories or read to her until Michi fell asleep. When Michi slept, Tomiko looked at her and always felt herself newly reminded of Nagayuki. Nagayuki's narrow, oval face became increasingly prominent, and on Michi's skin lay the same dull shimmer which Nagayuki's face had when first his beard came in fuzzily.

In her sleep Michi always pushed out her lower lip a little, as she often did during the day when one of her wishes was not granted. When she pouted in this way, it was a sign to Tomiko that within the next hour Michi would break something. The easiest way to prevent the pout was to quickly give Michi a present. It need only be some little thing—a piece of rice candy, a square of sweet bean jelly, or a paper fan with which she cooled herself in exactly the same way she had seen Father Hayato do it.

Rin had begun to keep such small presents for Michi handy in the kitchen, hidden away; for when Michi was in one of her sulky moods, Rin was the one who generally was made to pay for it. When no one was looking, Michi would take a chopstick from the drawer and lay it across the sill into the kitchen so that it looked as if it had been dropped by accident. Then she happily ran around the room, in the process stepping on the chopstick and cracking it. If Rin scolded her, she spoke in the same tone of voice Father Hayato used at times when he was reprimanding Rin. "Silence. I do not wish to hear another word about it."

182

Should Tomiko—who had often closely watched Michi's careful preparations step by step—scold the little girl, Michi, sobbing, threw herself on the tatami mats and kicked her legs so vigorously and persistently that, at the beginning, Tomiko simply left the house to escape having to endure more of Michi's obstinate screaming. Once outside, most of the time she could hear Michi very quickly stopping her sulky crying. But when Tomiko returned to the house after a while, even more chopsticks and sometimes even porcelain bowls had been broken.

In Father Hayato's presence, Michi was a totally different child. She never pouted or willfully destroyed anything. Father Hayato made it a rule to bring her a gift whenever he returned from town—a picture book, paints and brushes, glass balls, brightly colored origami paper.

One time, without any particular occasion, Father surprised Michi with a large dollhouse containing a completely furnished toy kitchen with stove, pots, and dishes, with a dining room and a bedroom as well as a bath with a proper wooden tub. He liked to have Michi play with her dollhouse in the back room. Even when he spent his daily hour in Noh recitation, he did not object to Michi's being in the room. But she had to keep quiet during this time.

Michi constantly sought his company and snuggled against him. When she came in from playing outside, she took off her soiled clothes without having to be reminded by Tomiko or Rin. She washed up in the bathroom, and then, quite naked or wearing only a pair of underpants, she went to Father Hayato and said with great self-confidence, "I'm clean."

This was an invitation for him to pull her close and pet her. Often, when the days were cooler, he sent her away, saying, "Put on some clothes," or he ordered her to crawl under his dull black silk wrapper which on such days he wore over his olive-green or dark-blue house kimono. She snuggled into it and was happy if she was allowed to go on sitting there while he prepared his powdered tea.

183

Her bright, attentive eyes followed his every movement, although she had watched the same ritual hundreds of times. Her head with its tousled hair nodded in time with the deft motions with which Father Hayato beat the mixture of harsh-smelling, bright-green tea powder and a tiny amount of hot water into a foam in the irregularly shaped ceramic bowl. Then she watched as he used a circular motion to guide a whisk made of a piece of bamboo that had been split open in a number of places along the side of the bowl, to shake off the last foam of foam and tea with a brief swirl.

Rin brought in the iron teakettle. As always, she apologized to Father Hayato for having taken so long. She put the kettle on the warming plate that was a part of the tea service. Carefully, so as not to bump into Michi, who was leaning against him, the father prepared his tea with the sure movements that had gained a certain independence through his decades-long use of the strictest forms of the tea ceremony. For the time it took for him to beat the tea into a foam, he required absolute silence in the room.

Then, after he had emptied his bowl in three sips, he said, without looking at Tomiko, "It has been eight months since we have had word from Nagayuki. I have the feeling that he will never amount to anything." In the silence that followed his words, he spoke again. "Six years is a long time." He fell silent and thoughtfully observed the empty tea bowl he was holding between his hands, turning it slowly this way and that. "Other men," he finally said, "do not need so much time to return dressed in brocade. In that amount of time they have won renown in America, so that they are invited to return there time and again."

Father Hayato reached for the hot iron kettle and carefully, to avoid any splash that could fall on Michi, poured water into his tea bowl. He rinsed out the bamboo whisk in it and brushed off the traces of foam clinging to the edge.

While he poured the cleaning water into the vase-shaped receptacle standing ready and finally wiped out the tea bowl with the small white cloth, he said with increasing force, "Not to write a single letter in eight months—that is abnormal for someone who at one time intended to be a good yōshi. Obviously he is not ill—at least he was not ill when Mr. Eda took the trouble to look him up. At least it is reassuring to know someone here in Himari who has visited Nagayuki in America and who, on the basis of his own experience, can judge how well Nagayuki has done by now. And Mr. Eda found him well."

26

For a couple of weeks, Father Hayato had not summoned a rickshaw when he wanted to go into town. He walked. For some weeks, too, he had not bought any more kimonos, and even the gifts he brought Michi had become increasingly inexpensive. Tomiko understood that the last of the money Nagayuki had sent almost three-quarters of a year ago was used up. They were even running low on the expensive powdered tea.

Wordlessly Father Hayato, holding Michi's hand, left the house. Rin had gone to visit her parents at the harbor, and Gen was in school. It was then that Tomiko saw Fumiya, shoulders hunched, hurry down the street. Tomiko quickly ran down the ladder to greet Fumiya at the front door.

"Perhaps it would be better if I come upstairs with you," Fumiya suggested.

"No, please stay here. The ladder is too steep for you."

"I'm not so old yet." Fumiya smiled.

"All the same, I wouldn't like you to slip on the ladder. It

186

really is steep. We will be undisturbed down here as well now," Tomiko replied. She put on water for tea.

Tomiko sensed that Fumiya had come on an urgent errand. She seemed deeply disturbed. "There are many rumors in town about Nagayuki. You must be careful. Someone wishes you ill," she blurted out even before she touched her teacup. "Do you know about it? Have you heard that in town they're saying that Nagayuki is sitting on a street corner in San Francisco, dressed in rags, begging? They say that he is so used to being kicked that he feels thankful for every kick that isn't dealt him."

Fumiya reported that in one store she had stood behind two women who had spoken of Nagayuki in the most venomous manner. They said that he was living like a rat in a dark lean-to house and that at night he ransacked garbage cans for discarded bits of food. When the women caught sight of Fumiya, they hurriedly changed the subject.

She had also heard people talking in the post office, without mentioning any name, but quite obviously the subject was Nagayuki again. When they noticed her, their chatter stopped.

"Someone is behind it—someone who has an interest in harming you and Nagayuki," Fumiya repeated.

"Eda is the one," Tomiko said, composed. She told Fumiya that Eda had been in this very room, sitting on the same pillow Fumiya was sitting on now.

"How did Eda manage to gain entry?" Fumiya asked. "I thought your father felt nothing but contempt for him."

"He used his marriage to Rin's sister as the pretext for a courtesy call. Very elegant, dressed all in white, he stood at the door and cast his bait—that on his last visit to America, he had called on Nagayuki in San Francisco."

"Then what?" Fumiya asked breathlessly as Tomiko faltered.

"Then, of course, he was invited to come in and have a cup of tea."

"What did he say about Nagayuki?"

"Not much while he was here, in the room. Just that Nagayuki was well and sends his regards. But chiefly he gave us to understand how easy it is if one has a great name behind one to pick the dollars off the trees in America. All it takes is a bit of self-discipline. Then, right here, he was served the best powdered tea with every formality."

While Tomiko spoke, Fumiya shrank more and more, finally appearing thin and small. Her hands, their backs traced with bluish veins beneath the thin skin, lay lifeless in her lap, as if made of white porcelain. "How could it have happened?" she stammered.

"It's all my fault," Tomiko confessed. "I let it slip that Nagayuki is in San Francisco. It was stupid of me."

"He could have found out some other way," Fumiya tried to console her.

"All the same. My going to his house to ask about the cheap fare aroused his attention. I was stupid. His nose is very sharp, and it doesn't take him long to smell out the rotten fish. It was then that Nagayuki stopped writing to me. And he hasn't sent me the ticket yet, either."

"But both of us know that Nagayuki needs time to save up the money for the passage," Fumiya said reassuringly. "It is more important to start thinking about how you will get away from Himari just as soon as the ticket does get here."

Her own words quickly restored Fumiya's animation. Her hands regained their mobility, and her shoulders straightened. "Go get a piece of paper," she said in her firm and reasonable way. "We'll make a list of everything you have to take with you when you leave here in a hurry."

Tomiko noted down a number of things she would absolutely have to take to Nagayuki. Everything that he used to like to eat. For herself, two or three plain kimonos would do, she thought, and some aprons because she was certain to have to go to work at once in San Francisco. Then Tomiko crossed the kimonos off her list altogether; she would sew Western dresses for herself. Hadn't Nagayuki written that in San Francisco all the women wore Western clothing?

"They will notice if you suddenly start sewing dresses for

yourself," Fumiya objected at once. "You had better take your most expensive kimonos with you. I'll inquire about where in Tokyo they'll give you the best price for them. By the way, what will you do about Michi?"

For a long time Tomiko stared into space without speaking. Finally she shook her head. "I won't be able to take her with me. Nagayuki needs all my energy. I don't know exactly how, but I'm certain I'll be able to help him earn money. It will be easier by myself than with Michi. Then we can come back that much sooner."

Then Tomiko fetched her secret bankbook and showed Fumiya how much had accumulated.

"There is enough there for your trip to Tokyo. I'll add as much as I can to it, so that you can live in Tokyo until your passport is issued. It will take a month. And don't forget to go to the Bureau of Families in good time—you'll need the transcript from the family ledger to apply for the passport. For a visa, you need confirmation of your marriage to Nagayuki; otherwise you will not be allowed to enter America."

After the completed list lay before them on the table, the old worry began to gnaw at Tomiko again. Nagayuki had not written for nine months.

"It must be nine months ago, too, that this man Eda was in San Francisco," Tomiko began anew. "Might he have told Nagayuki that the old Hayato mansion and all the grounds were lost long ago?"

"That would not be sufficient reason for Nagayuki's silence," Fumiya said decidedly. "In that case, he would have written all the sooner."

"That's what I thought, too," Tomiko murmured.

"What words can that man have used to threaten Nagayuki so that he stopped writing?" Fumiya said as if to herself, only half-aloud.

But before she could spin out the thought, Father Hayato, still holding Michi, came through the door. Without haste, Fumiya reached for the list which lay open on the table, making it vanish into her kimono sash. Michi, to whom Fumiya was a stranger, plucked at the father's sleeve. "Who is that lady?"

Father Hayato released Michi's hand and went to the center of the room, where there were other floor pillows. Carefully he smoothed his kimono and sat down. In greeting, he returned Fumiya's bow.

"We are worried about Nagayuki," Tomiko said quickly, to forestall any questions.

"Many lies are being told about him in the town," Fumiya added.

Father Hayato assumed his upright position and, still seated, supported both hands, fingers lightly spread, on his thighs. His eyes, shadowed by the bushy white brows, wandered searchingly over Fumiya and Tomiko. "I have heard the talk," he finally said, his voice mild, "but I attach no importance to it. Maturity gives us the strength to walk through the disagreements and storms of life without the impulse to jump into action. In this way the real truth is increasingly revealed. I will form my own judgment."

"Nagayuki is not well," Fumiya said. "Although I am only his mother and Nagayuki has been granted the honor of being received as a son in the Hayato family, I am taking the liberty of voicing the request that Tomiko be allowed to join Nagayuki." Fumiya clothed her words in all the caution she possessed. She spoke in a soft voice and with politely downcast eyes.

Years had passed since Father Hayato and Fumiya had last spoken to each other. The rare occasions when they did chance to meet had passed with the exchange of a very few polite phrases. Fumiya had never forgotten the end of the vehement confrontation between them in the tea room of the large old Hayato mansion shortly before Nagayuki's departure. Her rage, kindled that day, still burned in her. "I am speaking as a mother," she added softly now, "and in the certain knowledge that Nagayuki needs Tomiko's presence."

Father Hayato nodded in agreement. "Six years is a very long time, during which it is easy for anxiety to crest to a mighty wave. But I have practiced patience and waited for Nagayuki's return with a pure heart. From year to year. Without pressing. When his return was delayed, the understanding grew in me that Nagayuki might, after all, need a period of ripening, like a sickly tree that will bear fruit in the end. The fruit produced late is all the sweeter."

Fumiya, who was calmly gazing at Father Hayato while he spoke, compared his face with the Noh mask hanging on the wall behind him. On entering the room, she had noticed the mask at once and had grasped its many-leveled expression. At first glance it seemed to be the mask of an old man, but as soon as one looked at it for longer than the time of one deep breath, an expression of timeless youthfulness came to the fore. Suddenly it took on demonic features before hazily transforming itself back into the mask of an old man.

"I have never harbored a tinge of reproach," Father Hayato said calmly. "With a pure heart I thought only of the banquet I would prepare for Nagayuki when at last he returned dressed in brocade."

Tomiko could not restrain herself any longer. "But whenever Nagayuki sent money, he wrote that I should use it to join him. He needs me. Don't you understand?"

Father Hayato did not acknowledge Tomiko's outburst. "Others have gone to America alone, even without a Todai diploma, which opens every important door. Without a multitude of kimonos of a splendor to attract any observer. But they do not cut such poor figures today."

"You have no idea what difficulties Nagayuki had to contend with," Tomiko interrupted him sharply. "Alone in America."

Father Hayato waited with quiet patience for Tomiko to stop speaking. Then he said sorrowfully, "You are familiar with the old saying that if a samurai stumbles seven times, he gets back on his feet eight times. If Nagayuki were a true samurai, strong of heart and unshakable, he would not be vanquished by adversity in America. On the contrary, he would triumph over everything that threatens him. But perhaps Nagayuki is not a samurai at heart. He has not brought honor to the name of Hayato."

"Nagayuki is too noble and too sensitive to assert himself against ruthless people," Tomiko said, looking at her father with anger. "All those who have ever returned dressed in brocade won their money in America by brutality and gangsterism. I must join him. I must. To protect him."

An indulgent smile spread over Father Hayato's peaceful, wise face. "It's been a long time since I have seen you so angry," he said, and for an instant he closed his eyes. "It seems as if it were yesterday. I can still see you before me, little Tomiko-chan, always so willful. But now my Tomiko is a big girl, and she knows very well that a samurai does not depend on the help of a woman."

Michi, who had been standing by, a little intimidated, her mouth wide open in astonishment, listening incomprehending to the conversation, snuggled up to Father Hayato. He put his arm around her. "I've got something for you later," he said to her, his voice warm and gentle. "A very special snack of bean jelly."

Only then did he turn back to Fumiya. "It would be a grave error to take Nagayuki's unbroken silence, which has lasted more than eight months, as a good omen. In view of the uncertainty in which it places us, it would be irresponsible of me to send Tomiko to America now. I have long been chewing on the worrisome question of whether I overestimated Nagayuki's ability to dress himself in brocade. As long as I cannot be certain that Tomiko can lead the carefree life I want for her in America, I—her father—must not allow her to travel there."

Father Hayato indicated that he considered these words an end to the interview.

"I beg you to excuse me," he said, turning to Fumiya. With a strange weariness he rose to his feet and went to the back room.

 **27**

"I don't like the way Eda constantly tells everyone that he is my uncle," Gen said after he had won the Eda Cup in judo. "Wherever I go, he comes up to me and places his sweaty hand on my shoulder. Then, afterward, a lot of people say I didn't win the cup honestly. They say my cup is an uncle cup."

Gen turned the silver trophy to look at the inscription with hostile, covetous eyes. "I was the best judo fighter long before Eda married into our family. Why is he always seeking me out even though he doesn't understand the first thing about judo? All he is is rich, and the man who donated the judo hall. Is it my fault that he became my uncle?"

Tomiko looked up from her sewing, which she had taken up again recently. "No," she said to him warmly. "No, it is not your fault in any way. You and I, we know that you won the cup by your own efforts. That's all that counts—don't you agree?"

Gen beamed a little. "Will your dress be finished soon?" he asked Tomiko.

"Yes, tomorrow."

"I think the dress is beautiful. I like the color."

"I do, too. I'm fond of the purple and the big white flower pattern."

"I won't tell a soul about it," Gen reassured her, lightly touching the material. "Are you going to wear the dress in America?"

"Yes. When the ship puts into San Francisco harbor, I will be wearing it, so that Nagayuki will spot me from afar."

"I want to go with you."

"Later. Perhaps you'll come to America later."

"Will you write to me?"

"I will send you many postcards, so that you'll always know where I am."

"But . . . if you send me postcards, the others will also find out where you are," Gen said, suddenly worried.

"Once I get to America, there is nothing anyone can do to me. People are free there. And besides, Nagayuki will be there to help me."

Gen had become Tomiko's confidant. He alone knew that when no one was at home—not even Michi—she secretly sewed Western dresses for herself in the upper room. He had been initiated into her plans for flight. When Tomiko wanted to send word to Fumiya, she sent Gen, and Fumiya intercepted Gen at his school whenever she had a message for Tomiko.

"You know what I noticed?" Gen said, changing the subject again. "Eda comes near me only when I'm with other people. When I'm by myself, he pays no attention to me. But no sooner am I standing with someone else than he comes over and puts his damp hand on my shoulder. Then he talks to me as if he'd known me since I was a baby."

"He wants to be seen with you," Tomiko replied while she continued sewing carefully. "He knows that you have now officially become the son of Hayato, and that is why he wants to bask in your light."

194

"Before my name was Hayato, I was already a son of Hayato. My mother told me."

"But now it is legal, don't you see? Now your mother's name is Hayato, too. And thus Eda has become directly related to Hayato. Quite officially. That was his aim, after all."

"What does he get out of it?" Gen wanted to know.

Tomiko explained, "The name of Hayato has a ring to it because it is a samurai name with a great historical past. For many people, that means more than riches and wealth. Money can be quickly acquired in many ways. But not an old name."

"I do not ever want to be a samurai, and never rich," Gen protested. "Just rich enough to go to America. I wonder if they have different seashells there than we have here."

"I will write and tell you." Tomiko smiled at him. "And when you're grown up, you can come and visit me. We'll go to the beach together and look for shells."

"That's fine," Gen said, setting down his judo cup in the corner. "Is it true, by the way, that the other night Eda paid for the big banquet?" he asked after some thought.

"I don't know," Tomiko answered evasively. She hesitated, wondering if she should burden Gen with everything she had found out or suspected. After all, he was only fourteen years old and would have to spend at least four more years—perhaps even six—in Himari, depending on what he would do when he left school. It was his fond desire to become a teacher of biology. But his future hinged to a large extent on how well he managed to get through the time alone. At the great banquet he had sat at the head of the long table, between Father Hayato and Eda. He had looked very lost.

Eda repeatedly mentioned that Gen's resemblance to Father Hayato was truly astonishing to anyone seeing the two of them sitting side by side. Eda also said that it had been high time for Hayato to legally recognize Gen as his son. At least he hinted as much—more than once—and looked sharply at the mayor to see whether he had correctly interpreted Eda's insinuations.

Though Tomiko could not see the mayor, the faces of the other guests who sat in the same row as Eda and across from the mayor told her that Eda's words had met with general agreement. All night long Nagayuki was not mentioned by so much as a single word. All the more care did Eda take that everyone nodded when he characterized Gen as the only true son of Hayato, who on the basis alone of his surprisingly strong physical resemblance to Father Hayato and also because of his outstanding achievements in judo was already predestined to carry on the samurai spirit of the family. Eda dominated the evening in every way, although the occasion for the banquet was the official recognition of Rin as Hayato's new wife.

Rin, whose pillow was at the lower end of the seating order, across from Tomiko, sat with downcast eyes. Thus, without meaning to, she impressed everyone as a very good, devoted wife. She barely touched any food, while the guests, among them several town councillors and the mayor, helped themselves lavishly. The men were only too happy to have the waitress refill their sake bowls, and they grunted contentedly when the owner of the restaurant came in once and, bowing to the ground, inquired whether everything was as they wished. Father Hayato, in the seat of honor before the tokonoma recess, nodded condescendingly and dismissed him with a simple motion of the hand borrowed from the Noh repertoire.

"We must do something to assure the greatness of Himari," Eda shouted to the assembled company when the mood had become sufficiently animated. Eagerly he kept refilling Father Hayato's sake bowl and tried to persuade Gen to drink some more. But Gen had not even emptied his first bowl, and when Eda quickly filled it to the brim, he left it sitting untouched. Occasionally he stole a glance at Tomiko or at Rin's father, who sat on the other side of Eda, next to a town councillor. Confused by so much honor, Rin's father drank too much sake much too quickly. He was the first to keel over and fall asleep on the tatami matting.

Michi could not stand it very long by Tomiko's side. She

wanted to run all around the room in her party kimono. She discovered Rin's father sleeping on the tatami mats. Michi took off and, shrieking with pleasure, jumped over him. Only when Father Hayato caught her, tenderly put his arm around her, and whispered something in her ear did she give up her game and return quietly to the women's end of the table and take her place next to Tomiko. There she nestled on her floor pillow and soon fell asleep among the chatting, joking, laughing company.

"We must do something to make Himari great," Eda repeated loudly. Pausing briefly for effect, he added, "I have a suggestion."

All came to attention. Suddenly even the scurrying of the serving maids seemed an interruption. Eda leaned forward and, over Gen's head, whispered with Father Hayato. Finally Father Hayato nodded, and Eda sat back upright. Tomiko saw that a triumphant smile had spread over his features, although he tried to suppress it with a serious mien. Eda waited until one of the town councillors encouraged him by calling out, "What is your proposition, Mr. Eda?"

"It's true that our town is not rich," Eda began. "We lack an industry, and our agriculture, too, is not very developed. The countryside around here is too mountainous, and the ocean cannot feed us all. The only thing of value we possess is the beauty of our location and"—he cleared his throat suggestively—"and our love of Himari."

Everyone nodded in agreement, either to themselves or to each other, until someone else asked a question. "What is your proposal, then?"

"We have one other possession," Eda continued, tipping his knuckle against his temple. "Our heads . . ."

Everyone grinned.

". . . and we must use them to lead Himari to prominence."

Tomiko admired the cleverness with which Eda irresistibly drew everyone's attention to himself, at the same time suggesting, by an occasional glance at Father Hayato, that the two of them were in this together. Father Hayato, impressive in the full splendor of his white hair, occupied the place of honor. His expression seemed removed from reality, almost like a Noh mask, bathed in dignity.

While all waited in suspense for the proposal, they thought only Eda would find a simple way out of the poverty of their town, Eda finally brought forth his proposition. He pointed out that it was on the beautiful large estate of the honorable old house of Hayato that by far the most productive hot spring flowed from the rocks. It practically offered itself for the establishment of a spa with baths and massage rooms. The lordly Hayato mansion, with its many rooms, could easily be turned into a hotel with a separate restaurant. Perhaps a subsidiary building, he added with a sly grin, could serve as a geisha house.

Before questions could be raised concerning the cost of such a project, Eda pointed out that the influx of tourists from such cities as Kobe, Osaka, and Kyoto—which, if the other hot springs in Himari and its immediate surroundings were also put into use, could turn into a veritable flood of tourism—would result in an increase in passenger traffic that would fall wholly and entirely to Himari's sole passenger craft. Since the boat was the property of a private company, owned by seven or eight of the most important town councillors as well as the mayor of Himari, this argument immediately allowed Eda to blunt the point of any objections from this particular group. He assured himself of Father Hayato's goodwill by revealing, in a conspiratorial tone, that he had already spoken with the present owner of the Hayato property, who, as was well known, was a major industrialist from Tokyo. Eda had been told that he would be happy to return to the original owner this piece of property, which had come into his hands through a chain of unfortunate circumstances. Further, Eda hinted, he had it from a reliable source that Father Hayato would soon be in possession of a considerable sum of money—enough to make available about half the repurchase price of the old Hayato property. The remainder of the financing remained to be discussed. Perhaps the municipality of Himari could step into the breach.

When Tomiko heard Eda say that Father Hayato was expecting a significant sum of money, she stiffened in fear. Feverishly she wondered whether a letter from Nagayuki might have arrived recently. But for weeks now she had waited for the postman every day, and she had never left the house before she had not at least seen him pass by twice a day on his rounds when there was no mail for Hayato at all. The only possibility—so it went through her head—was that Father Hayato had intercepted the postman before he reached the house.

Gen had helped to watch, and presumably he suspected why Tomiko was determined to be the one to receive Nagayuki's next letter. But when Tomiko looked questioningly at Gen at the upper end of the round, she saw him, sitting between Eda and Father Hayato, his eyes large and helpless, fighting sleep.

Father Hayato nodded with satisfaction even as someone in the company raised his sake bowl and announced loudly, "Mr. Eda should become a town councillor."

"Oh, no," Eda called out, after a rapid glance around the assembly had assured him of agreement in all the faces. "I am not worthy of such an honor."

Promptly the view was voiced that since as of this day Eda was an official member of the Hayato family, it would be only proper to see him in the ranks of town councillors.

"No, no," Eda still refused, and motioned toward Father Hayato. "The head of the Hayato family and, as in all humility I may call him from now on, my honored family head also, alone is due the distinction of being a town councillor. I"—he bowed to the assembled group—"perhaps I could . . . if—but surely that is not the case—if it should be in the best interest of our town . . . assume the modest post of resort director."

"Yes, yes," several voices in the group called out. "That certainly is in the best interests of our town."

 **28**

Gen climbed the ladder to the upper room and told Tomiko that Fumiya wanted to speak to her urgently.

The ticket for the passage, Tomiko thought, hurrying.

"Did he send the ticket?" Tomiko asked when Fumiya led her into her room.

"No," Fumiya answered. "But I know why Nagayuki has not written for nine months."

"What is it? Has he been ill?" Tomiko could hardly wait to hear. "Come on, tell me what's the matter. Or did they put Nagayuki in prison? He's so gullible. Maybe he was tricked."

"The only thing of importance," Fumiya said in a calm voice, "is for you to keep your composure now. Here, read this." She handed Tomiko a letter that consisted of several closely written sheets.

The small, precise characters of Nagayuki's handwriting

blurred before Tomiko's eyes, and she had to hold on to Fumiya so she would not faint.

"Come, first sit down. I'll make you a cup of tea."

Tomiko saw that the letter was addressed to Fumiya, not to herself. This gave her the first little stab.

Nagayuki was telling Fumiya that he had hesitated for a long time—for months—before taking up his brush once more, and he had made several starts, only to tear up the page again. But he considered it his duty to communicate to her—his real mother—after such long silence, why he had decided to remain in America and never return to Himari. Shame forbade his writing to Father Hayato, but she, as his real mother, would surely understand him.

When he thought of Himari, he wrote, it was not easy to keep his heart free from the resentments that had dominated his thoughts during recent months like the constant humming of flies. The only thing that still tied him to Himari was the feeling of esteem and love for Father Hayato. It was true that ever since joining the Hayato household he had lived in fear of the father's stringent moral demands, but at the same time Hayato's tranquillity and goodness had been a spur to his own achievements. In the last few years he had received only a few letters from Father Hayato himself, quite in contrast to the numerous missives from Tomiko, whose only aim it must have been to keep the truth from him.

Fumiya had returned and set the tea in front of Tomiko. Her features expressed a quiet, gentle grief as she watched Tomiko, facing her in silence. Tomiko repeatedly interrupted her perusal of the letter because she had to reread the lines, the sense of which she could not comprehend. When she came to the passage telling of Nagayuki's trials in the early years, Tomiko rubbed at her eyes several times.

Only a few days after arriving in San Francisco, Nagayuki wrote, he had made the painful discovery that nowhere in the city was there a place for someone like himself. Everywhere he had been shown the door. Finally he had been able to get hold of a few dollars by selling his kimonos in Chinatown. Just enough to keep his head above water for a couple of weeks because the weather was mild and he could spend his nights in the streets.

His subsequent work in a fish cannery in Alaska—under conditions about which he would prefer not to speak—had earned him a hundred and forty-five dollars. That was his pay for a whole season. Then he had hired out in the fruit orchards of California, where the hectic hours of bone-crushing labor were punctuated only by cuts from the whips of the mounted overseers. Nevertheless, there, too, he had done well through hard work and overtime, enabling him to send money to Himari.

He had worked in the orchards three summers; in the spring he had been hired for the sowing and weeding of the vegetables and in the fall for the fruit harvest. Often he had spent only a week in one place before going on to the next one, where they paid five cents a day more. He had spent four winters in San Francisco, performing the most menial chores, which fell mostly to the Japanese immigrants. During the days he worked in a laundry or was hauling garbage or looking for other paid employment, but at night he had read books and busied himself increasing his knowledge of American law, with the aim of someday being truly useful to the untold thousands of Japanese immigrants. Most of them were helpless at the hands of the white farmers and their Japanese overseers. There was no one to whom they could turn for advice, for they were protected by no American law. As far as the Japanese consulate people in San Francisco were concerned, they were no more than dirt, best swept into the gutter.

Often he had to resist temptations that would have brought him easy money. "At such moments I always remembered that through Hayato I became the son of a samurai," Nagayuki wrote, "and therefore committed to being true to myself and the reputation of my name."

For two winters he had swept up a theater after the nightly performances. On this job he had repeatedly found money, once even a five-dollar bill. But he had always returned it to the theater owner, thus earning a reputation for being a trustworthy, honest Japanese.

"Otherwise," Nagayuki's letter continued, "I would not now be a translator at the Court and a legal adviser. Though I owe my present respectable position and my financial livelihood—secure at last—to the friendly recommendations of white people whose trust I won, I know in my heart that without the shining model of Father Hayato I would never have been capable of this achievement. All the deeper is the feeling of shame which drains me and eats away at my innards when I think what Tomiko is up to in my absence. I wondered for a long time why she never came to join me, although time and again I begged her to. Every time I sent money for her fare, I counted the days that still had to pass before she would arrive. Time and again I stood at the pier in the harbor when a ship from Yokohama was making fast, bringing passengers. But Tomiko was never among them. She never wrote to me why she did not come but filled her pages with meaningless trifles which, in my longing for her, could only hurt me. In spite of all my despair, each time I began to save all over again. When the year was over and the winter in San Francisco began, I sent more than enough money for her passage, and again I stood at the pier many times and many hours. Now that I know her true nature, I feel nothing but an unspeakably deep pity for Father Hayato who, as I heard from Mr. Eda, now has snow-white hair from grief at so much shame.

"For long I struggled not to believe what Eda told me. Even when three other Japanese men came to me and unanimously reported that when their ships lay in the harbor of Himari, they had heard of Tomiko as a prostitute known all over town and had themselves had her in their cabins, everything in me struggled against lending credence to their words, for there may be a woman in the harbor of Himari who is also called Tomiko. I asked these men for proof that it was my Tomiko. They only laughed and said that I'd get my proof for certain.

"I knew one of these Japanese from my working days in the orchards, and I mistrusted him profoundly. In the meantime, he had become rich through a gambling casino and a dockside restaurant with rooms by the hour, which he opened here in San Francisco. Many of the former overseers and slave drivers enter these businesses, or they open bathhouses. I don't know if this man recognized me also. I, at least, knew as soon as I saw him that he had been the overseer on the George Russell Apricot Farm who had been ruthless and cruel in spurring the workers on with the whip, high on his horse. That is why I lent no credence to his words.

"But then another man told me that he had met Tomiko in Tokyo and spent a whole night with her. He even named the hotel and the price he had paid Tomiko for the night. Since I did not believe him—I shouted at him that all these years Tomiko had never been to Tokyo, I was quite certain—he answered coolly that I could check with the Ike-no-Chaya Hotel whether she had spent the night there on a particular date.

"I wrote to the hotel, for I am familiar with it from my Todai days. It is situated between the Ueno Park and the university, and when Tomiko and I were first married and had not yet found a home of our own in Tokyo, we lived for two weeks at the Ike-no-Chaya. We were very happy there.

"Yesterday I received an answer from the hotel. They told me that Tomiko had indeed spent the night there on the date I had mentioned. Tomiko had to pick that hotel of all places to meet another man!

"I understand very clearly that now, when Father Hayato suffers great financial need, Tomiko takes money from men in exchange for her body, for her father can no longer provide her with the luxuries she has been used to from childhood. That is why she so urgently wishes to leave Himari, and asked me for the ticket—because here in San Francisco, among so many womenless Japanese men, she expects still greater profit from her base appetites."

Tomiko's hands dropped. The pages of Nagayuki's letter slid from her fingers and fell from her lap to the tatami mats.

"There isn't much time left," Fumiya said in a cool voice which could not conceal her own emotional turmoil. "Not much time to think. Reproaches—and especially self-reproaches—are not appropriate now. We must talk about what to do next."

Tomiko, glassy-eyed, stared straight ahead, and seemed not to hear Fumiya's words.

Fumiya shook her arm. "I know what you are feeling. And you can imagine that as his mother I . . ." With the back of her hand she wiped her eyes, and with a jerk she straightened her head and her back.

"Listen to me," she said, shaking Tomiko with both hands. "This is no time for tears. You must get a passport and a visa in the fastest possible way. For the passport application, you first need the transcript from the family ledger, so that you can prove you are Nagayuki's wife. Otherwise they will ask you at the passport office for formal consent from Father Hayato. You'd best to go today to the Bureau of Families and get the transcript. Tomorrow you will go to the prefectural capital."

"Why?" Tomiko asked, her voice flat and colorless.

"Because it takes four weeks for you to get your passport. I have made inquiries. The normal waiting period is three months, but the foreign ministry in Tokyo can speed it up. Then you'll need a visa. For that you have to appear in person at the American consulate in Kobe. It is getting harder and harder from year to year to get a visa for America. But you needn't worry. You will get a visa because you are married. All you have to do is bring sufficient proof that Nagayuki is in America and that you are married to him. In any case, the excerpt from the family ledger again. That's important. As soon as you have the visa, which takes only a few days, you will get a ship directly in Kobe."

"What ship? Nagayuki doesn't want me anymore," Tomiko sobbed abruptly and buried her face in both hands.

"I will write him this very day," Fumiya said as firmly as possible, and she repeated her words until Tomiko looked at her with teary eyes.

"Really? Do you think he'll believe you?"

For a moment Fumiya was silent. Then a gentle, confident smile spread over her slowly aging face, and she rebuked Tomiko. "Don't you have any faith in a mother's promise? Just think why Nagayuki sent me this letter, after torturing himself for months. He wants me to tell him that the whole story is a lie."

Fumiya poured out the tea, which had grown cold, and brought hot water for more.

"One thing is certain," she said with cool deliberation. "Eda is having you watched. He even set his people on you in Tokyo. How else could he know the name of the hotel where you spent the night? Probably he even knows that you went to the foreign ministry and the American embassy. Weren't you aware that someone was following you?"

"No." Tomiko shook her head thoughtfully. "But I was not looking for it."

"This time we must be more careful. You mustn't even buy your own ticket to the prefectural capital. I shall buy it for you and slip it to you secretly. Tomorrow morning at eight o'clock at the railway station. At that hour there's such a crowd that one is not conspicuous. But you yourself must go to the Bureau of Families. If you hurry, you can still get the excerpt from the family ledger today."

"But Nagayuki won't send me a ticket now." Tomiko sobbed again. "Not after everything he wrote."

Fumiya put her arm around Tomiko's shoulders and wiped away her tears. "Don't worry," she said soothingly. "I shall buy you the ticket—believe me, I'll buy it for you."

"But you can't—"

"I don't have much that can be turned into cash, but I'm certain the name of Ogasawara still has enough luster for a bank loan."

"Really?" Tomiko asked, gazing in disbelief. "Do you really

206

think that will work? Will the bank give a loan to a woman?"

"I think so, yes." Fumiya nodded confidently, but her eyes revealed her deep apprehensiveness, which she managed to conceal only with great effort. Her narrow face had grown quite pointed and glowed with an almost unnatural agitation.

"As soon as I get to America, I will send the money back to you," Tomiko said, full of eagerness, and enclosed Fumiya's hand in both her own. Then she grew thoughtful again. "I don't understand any of it. Eda got what he wanted. The other day, at the banquet, they even spoke of making him resort director of Himari."

Tomiko told Fumiya about the evening when Rin's elevation to legal wife and Gen's recognition as the son of Hayato were celebrated, told her about the plan to transform the old Hayato property into a resort hotel with adjoining geisha house. Finally she repeated Eda's announcement that Father Hayato would shortly come into a sizable sum of money.

"It cannot possibly be coming from Nagayuki," Fumiya said.

"But who else?"

"Eda is tricky," Fumiya said, not hiding her admiration. "I've heard that he has been interested in the Hayato mansion for a long time. He was probably talking about his own money."

"Do you think he has that much?"

"It's possible. But clearly his money does not go so far as to buy the house altogether. In that case, what you told me is a particularly shrewd move. I must admit; the fellow is clever. Fortunately soon none of this will touch us any longer."

Fumiya urged Tomiko to leave. "Go now, so that you will not be too late at the Bureau of Families. The main thing is that your married state is documented, so that you can get your passport and your visa. In the meantime I'll see how I can arrange your ship's passage."

29

Tomiko's hands were damp as she paid the fee at the cashier's window and was handed the thin, rustling pages. She bowed slightly to the aging official, who was looking at her through thick glasses with a certain intimacy. "Hot today—don't you agree? We'll have a typhoon soon."

Tomiko sensed that he would like to inveigle her into a conversation. "Yes, it's likely," she said in a friendly tone and left quickly. As she walked out, pushing the carefully folded sheets into her kimono neckline, she suddenly felt strangely elated, yet empty at the same time. Tomorrow, without a word to her father, she would travel to the prefectural capital and fill out the passport application.

Tomiko hurried home. Even at a distance she could hear her father's voice. It came from the back room, and instinctively

Tomiko stopped for an instant to listen to the sound. Father was reciting a Noh passage Tomiko had not heard from him in a long time. All the shojis in the house stood wide open to let the slightest breath of air into the house, but there was no breeze, and the mugginess stifled the whole town. The sky had become overcast by an even, gray haze, dulling the rays of the sun.

"The typhoon will be here soon," Rin shouted to Tomiko from the vegetable garden. "Maybe tomorrow."

"Psst!" Tomiko signaled to Rin for silence. She did not want Father to become aware of her return.

Startled, Rin placed her hand, soiled with garden dirt, to her mouth. She nodded vigorously to show that she understood.

Tomiko approached the house on tiptoe, and at the doorsill she removed her shoes. Through the open shoji she saw her father sitting before the low music stand. He had his back to her, so that he could see the rear section of the garden, where he had placed most of his bonsai trees at the beginning of the hot season.

Michi sat snuggled against Father. Tomiko smiled to see the little girl sitting with her arms around her knees, her face serious, staring into the garden with as much dignity as Father.

Tomiko listened to the oddly wailing melody of the Noh chant. Seeming to come from a great distance, Father's voice swelled to fill the whole room, just as the sound of the foghorn covers the whole bay at night, when benighted ships felt their way into the harbor of Himari, or as the wind begins to sing when it became caught in rocky fissures. These same melancholy sounds, rising and waning, are heard at such times, and they are said to be the laments of the fishermen who went out to sea never to return.

Not for a long time had Tomiko been so deeply stirred by her father's Noh chanting. Even the features of the mask on the wall seemed to her more benign than ever before. In the shadowless light preceding the typhoon, the mask had lost its grimness, and a hint of wistfulness tinged its features.

Motionless, Tomiko stood in the doorway, holding her shoes, which she intended carrying upstairs to keep her return a secret. She looked over at Father and at Michi, who was still leaning against him. Father's back had grown round, and his hair was as white as the white of a distant cloud.

Abruptly Tomiko realized that she would miss this picture— the sound of Father's voice, Michi, sitting so still, though usually bubbling over with her love of life. I'll miss Michi, Tomiko thought, and I'll miss the years of seeing her expectant eyes when I tell her a story at night before she goes to sleep. I'll miss her gentle breathing as she sleeps, her horrid grinding of her teeth that she still hasn't stopped, and her pouty expression which she won't put on when Father is present. I won't stay away long, Tomiko whispered silently. She had to tear herself away from the spot where she was standing.

While she crept through the room as silently as possible, she felt the mask's eyes follow her steps. On the ladder to the upper room, she was overcome with the fear that it was wrong to leave her father so suddenly. She did not dare turn around and take another look at the mask. Somewhere deep in her soul she regretted the need to turn away from her father. At the same time she was glad that he no longer held any power over her.

Gen knelt at the top of the ladder and stretched out a helping hand to Tomiko. She signaled to him to keep quiet, and he responded with a conspiratorial smile. When Tomiko was about to go to her pillow, he pulled her by the sleeve to his corner of the room. "A man from Osaka was here with a big automobile," he whispered into her ear. "He even let me sit behind the steering wheel." Gen beamed with pride, expecting Tomiko to admire him. But Tomiko only patted his face lightly, and said softly and hastily, "How nice for you." Then she fled over to her corner. Carefully she pulled the transcript from the family ledger out of her kimono.

"The steamship ticket?" Gen asked so softly that his words

were almost drowned in Father's Noh chant which rose from below in a strangely distorted modulation.

"No." Tomiko smiled at him. "Not yet." Father Hayato's voice sounded dusky, as if filtered through leafy thickets which swallowed the more brightly colored notes and let only the deep tones penetrate. Tomiko unfolded the pages of rustling, thin paper and carefully scrutinized the characters entered on it in a scratchy, black clerical penmanship. She had never before held such a document. Each page was resplendent with the chief official's red seal, applied at the bottom to testify to the correctness of the transcript. While Tomiko went over each line, beginning with the earliest copied entry, stating Father's birth-date, an automobile came to a stop before the house.

Sono's loud voice with its unmistakable drawling Osaka accent rang out. "Here I am, back again," he shouted into the house. "A real scorcher today, isn't it?"

Gen pulled at Tomiko's sleeve. "That's him—that's the man with the automobile. He came back."

He gave Tomiko a questioning look. She saw that he wanted to go downstairs. Do you need me to stay? his eyes begged. Tomiko shook her head, but reminded Gen by putting her finger to her lips that he was not to give away her presence. "Agreed," Gen nodded and went down the ladder nimbly.

Tomiko paid little attention to Sono's loud voice rising upward and extinguishing Father's Noh chant. She turned back to the transcript.

"I've been to the bank," Sono's voice called out. "Luckily, my money had already arrived. Look here, in my briefcase. The sight of all those beautiful banknotes can't help but make one's heart leap with joy. All neatly bundled, as is proper for a broker who knows his place."

Tomiko could not understand Father Hayato's answer. It seemed strange to her to imagine Father peering into a briefcase stuffed with naked bundled banknotes.

Tomiko had come to the entry of her own birth. She counted back: twenty-seven years ago. It was followed immediately with the notation of Nagayuki's entrance into the Hayato family as its yōshi. Full information about the Ogasawaras followed. Fumiya's birthdate was also entered. Oh, is that how old she is, Tomiko thought. Her mind wandered back to the day, ten years ago, when she had married Nagayuki. The transcript from the family ledger reduced the event down to two sober lines.

Tomiko was annoyed by Sono's noisy cheerfulness in the room below. She would have liked to call down for him to lower his voice. But Sono was laughing and clearly in a good mood. "I'm so glad that we agreed on the price so quickly. There's always some doubt in the case of a divorced woman. But in this case . . ."

Tomiko was taken aback as she scanned the final entries in the family ledger. Michi's birth was entered, then Mother's death, then the marriage between Father and Rin and the recognition of Gen as a son of Hayato. But then an entry noted that the head of the Hayato family had requested the removal of Nagayuki's name from the family ledger. The request was repeated word for word. "Due to behavior demonstrably damaging to the family," read the craggy black clerical script, "the elimination of the yōshi's name is officially registered."

The characters blurred before Tomiko's eyes, dissolving into disparate inkblots. She felt the thin, flimsy paper grow infinitely heavy in her hands, pulling her arms and her body to the ground. She read the lines once more, running her finger along the rows of characters. As long as she had not come to the end of the last line, with the official red seal, she struggled against accepting the official truth listed there. Then her resistance collapsed. The realization that Father had cast out Nagayuki and broken her marriage to him infused her like molten lead.

Sono's loud voice forced its way into her thoughts over and over. Slowly Tomiko understood that she was a divorced woman. And that she was the divorced woman Sono was talking about.

"Isn't the beautiful daughter at home?" Sono's impatient voice could be heard from downstairs.

Father called Rin.

Then Gen spoke, quickly and loudly. "No, she has gone out."

Rin answered, "Yes, she is upstairs."

When Rin came to the top of the ladder, she found Tomiko sunk forward. Frightened, she rushed to her side and touched her. "What's the matter?"

Gen, who had followed her at once, whispered, "Leave her alone. She doesn't want to come downstairs."

Rin tried to raise Tomiko and pillowed Tomiko's head in her lap. "It's all because of the weather. Whenever there's a typhoon in the offing, the weather is unbearable. I feel the same way," Rin moaned.

"Leave her alone. Her hands are so cold," Gen begged softly.

"It's the weather," Rin insisted. "It makes me come weak all over, too, when the typhoon is coming." She brushed Tomiko's hair from her forehead and loosened her kimono sash so that she could breathe easier.

"Father called you," Rin was talking at Tomiko. "There is a visitor. A man. A rich man—he even has an automobile."

"But she doesn't want to go downstairs." Gen's voice was already beginning to be tinged with desperation.

"He's brought bride money," Rin continued emotionally, and started to fix Tomiko's hair. "I saw it myself when I brought in the tea. A whole briefcase full, a big one. Lots of bride money."

When Gen pushed away Rin's hand and embraced Tomiko with all his might, Rin reproached him. "But Father called her." She began to dab Tomiko's face with powder. "You have to obey your father," she urged Tomiko. "He always means well."

"Leave her alone!" Gen hissed, fiery with rage. "She doesn't want to go downstairs." He brought his lips very close to Tomiko's ear and whispered to her, "Shall I go for help to the Ogasawaras?" Thereupon Tomiko shook her head almost imperceptibly.

Tomiko allowed Rin to raise her to her feet and tie her sash again. She let Rin lead her to the ladder. When she wavered, Gen also supported her and held her. Thus she went down the ladder with Rin's and Gen's help.

"There she comes, the beautiful daughter!" Sono shouted happily. "More beautiful than ever, and even more attractive than I remembered her."

Sitting, he bowed deeply to Tomiko, whom Rin had led to a floor pillow that had been hurriedly shoved into place.

"What a pity that a typhoon is coming up," Sono noted, thoroughly wiping away his perspiration with a large white cloth. He tucked it away again between his trousers and his shirt.

"What a bad month to call for a young wife!" He laughed richly at his own joke. "But when I got the news that I could come and fetch the beautiful daughter whenever it suited me, I couldn't stand another day in Osaka. Typhoon or no, I don't care. What a piece of good luck that I happened to have the bride money in liquid assets. In our profession, it is not always easy to have ready cash on hand."

Again he ended his words with a laugh. Giving every sign of satisfaction, he rubbed his hands. "It was worth it," he said, nodding at everyone in the room, even at Michi and Gen. He emptied his tea bowl, which Rin had filled up again.

Father Hayato was holding his long-stemmed fan and used it to cool himself. His motions held the same even calm and dignity as on other warm days, when there was no such oppressive humidity that clung to the skin.

Rin kneeled next to Tomiko, fanning her.

Father's kindly eyes rested on Tomiko. "This is a wonderful day, a day when you have come to the end of a long journey along the wrong road." With an elegant gesture, he laid the fan aside and picked up his tea bowl. "As numerous as pebbles, bitterness and thwarted hopes lay along your previous path. Each time I saw you sewing, my pain was deep and long-lasting. It is unworthy of the daughter of a samurai to sew far into the night on clothes for others. The years that have passed will take

214

their place in your spatial and temporal existence as a time of trial and maturation. You have proved yourself in your forbearing acceptance of the unexpected. In future you shall live without care, in a spacious home, surrounded by many servants, and you shall increasingly come near what is truly beautiful. How much have I wished such a life for my only daughter."

Sono nodded emphatically at these words and promised to indulge Tomiko in every respect. He had made a number of arrangements, he said. He had even had a tea chamber added to his house in Osaka. "I can already see the beautiful daughter, carrying out the tea ceremony in her pale loveliness."

Michi cuddled closer to Father Hayato. Her serious, astonished eyes examined Sono's round, bald skull and his reddish skin gleaming with perspiration.

"Your mama will return," Sono said to her. "There's no need for you to be sad. She'll bring you lots of toys from Osaka. What would you like? A great big ball? Or glass beads so you can make your own colorful necklace? Or a tricycle? I'll buy you everything you want." Sono put out his hand for the bursting black leather briefcase sitting between him and Father Hayato.

"If we hurry, we'll get to Osaka before the typhoon," he said and with a vigorous push he shoved the briefcase toward Father Hayato. "The bride money has been carefully counted. You can trust me."

"I trust you," Father Hayato answered with his kindly expression.

Finale

Thousands of points of light still danced and hovered before my eyes, strewn over the width of the bay of Himari. They flowed together, drifted apart, joined together again, turned into strips of light in the surging waves. I was enfolded in the warmth of the night. My clothes had dried on my body. Ceaselessly the narrow lines of foam crept up the sand, accompanied by the monotony of the rising and falling roar. As the waves receded, the foam spread into white carpets which were quickly sucked back up into the night. I thought that they were still there, the hundreds and hundreds of people who, like myself, had hurried to the beach in the evening to entrust their Obon boats to the sea. Even as the flotilla of lanterns headed for the mouth of the bay, carried on the ebb tide, they had stood there—silent shadows—and watched the journey of the souls.

> Return
> Next year
> Return . . .

The colors had long since faded, and the colorful multiplicity of the lanterns had merged into a ribbon of light gliding past the dark cliffs at the edge of the bay toward the open sea, as if drawn by the moon, which was waning toward the west.

> Return
> Next year
> Return . . .

Imperceptibly the change had come about. Where the ribbon of light had marked the Obon boats, now only the trembling reflections of the moon and the stars moved on the waves. Silently the beach had emptied, and when I looked up, there was no one else there. Only in the spots where the torches had burned, their remnants, black cudgels, rose from the pale sand.

There had been great eagerness and expectation when Naga-yuki returned, at last, after sixty years in America.

The covetous glances of his relatives clung to his five well-filled suitcases. Everyone vied for the honor of carrying one of them. They said, with self-conscious jocularity, that they must contain millions of dollars, or surely fat bundles of stocks and bonds . . . what with the weight of the cases . . . and after sixty years in America . . .

"Sixty years is long enough to gather a huge fortune. . . ."

"It's true that he looks seedy in his worn suit, but the suitcases . . ."

"He has returned dressed in brocade, and his modest appearance is only a clever dissimulation. . . ."

"I bet he brought back a fat bundle of dollars for each of us. . . ."

"All of us will be rich now. . . ."

I had never seen so many relatives all at the same time. Some of them were people I'd never met before, but they said they were Nagayuki's nieces and nephews. They looked at me out of the corners of their eyes and whispered to each other. I thought:

they worry that I, as Nagayuki's granddaughter, might get too large a share of the millions of dollars they think he has.

Later, when it turned out that the suitcases contained only old letters, photographs, some of them yellowed, diaries kept in precise handwriting for more than sixty years, and otherwise nothing but enough linens for his own use, all the relatives vanished in the quiet way peculiar to them.

The night had long since swallowed up the names of Nagayuki and Tomiko and extinguished the black characters on the white sails of my Obon boat. I looked over the empty beach and the ocean, which had grown desolate. The moon had tipped toward the cliffs at the mouth of the bay, abandoning the sky to the stars. All the space between me and the sinking width of the horizon was filled with the echo of souls.